The Last Thing Before
The Apocalypse

I0633815

Peter G. Mackie

chipmunkapublishing
the mental health publisher

Published by

Chipmunkapublishing

http://www.chipmunkapublishing.com

Copyright © Peter G. Mackie 2013

ISBN   978-1-84991-966-1

Chipmunkapublishing gratefully acknowledge the support of Arts Council England.

Author Biography

Peter G Mackie was born in Perth, Scotland in 1957 and, as a teenager, was mistakenly kept in the Adolescent Unit of a psychiatric hospital for two and a half years, an experience which affected his whole life and which led him to suffer from depression.

Due to problems with his family, he ran away from home at the age of 16 and suffered abuse on the streets of London.

At the age of 17, after a brief period in a hippy commune, he wrote his novel *The Madhouse of Love* in a bed-sit in Tooting, South London, based on his earlier experiences in the psychiatric unit.

From 1977 to 1984, he spent a period working and travelling in Europe, which helped him to see a different perspective on life.

However, due to unemployment in the 1980s, he was forced to return to Scotland, where he took an HND in Computer Data Processing, but failed to find work in that field.

Due to his education having been disrupted early in life, he has had to survive by doing unskilled jobs interspersed with periods of unemployment.

From 2001 to 2007, he went through a very difficult time, moving from place to place, trying to find work and accommodation, with little success, causing him to have a nervous breakdown and to lapse again into depression.

He ended up homeless in Edinburgh, where he sold *The Big Issue* for over a year.

In 2011, he completed an IT course at Redhall Walled Garden, a project in Edinburgh run by the Scottish Association for Mental Health (SAMH).

Between the 1970s and 1990s, he had poems published by numerous small press magazines.

He has also recorded a CD of music on piano and synthesiser *All Over the Shop*, which is available over the Internet.

In July 2012, he did some voluntary work with disadvantaged teenagers in Slovenia and is now planning to train to work with homeless young people in Edinburgh.

The Last Thing Before The Apocalypse

Faust Returns to the Fatherland

The events in this story took place many years ago now in a city full of bizarre goings-on which used to be divided by a wall and whose inhabitants seemed to have a split personality.

There will always be a corner of a foreign field where weirdos hang out from all over the world, the downtrodden, the poor in spirit, the poets and painters who died in the gutter, who have seen the best minds of their generation destroyed by madness, the sisters of mercy and the beautiful losers.....

*   *   *

One sultry afternoon, in the autumn of 1981, when Hamish, a young Scotsman, and his friend Jack were walking around Kreuzberg, Berlin, Jack found three bottles of wine dated "1952", "1955" and "1958" behind some derelict-looking office buildings, as if they had just been discarded after an office party.

They sat next to the rubbish bins and downed the first two bottles dated "1952" and "1955" between them. Then, Jack eyed the bottle marked "1958" and remarked, jokingly, "Oh, I don't usually go for 58's!", after which he smiled, uncorked the bottle and raised it to his lips.

Hamish, however, always refused to partake of any food that Jack had found while raking around in rubbish bins, which he would find him doing now and again.

Sometimes, at around this time, when he had been out with Jack and had had a bit to drink, Hamish would notice that he had just lit up a cigarette while another one was still burning in the ashtray. In fact, on one occasion, when he had just lit up a cigarette, he looked down at the ashtray and noticed that there were actually four cigarettes still left burning there.....

Another afternoon, they went to visit the offices of ***Bär Fax***, Berlin's only English language magazine, which had been started up by some mainly Irish and also one or two English people with whom they were acquainted. A middle-aged man, who turned out to be a Swede, but who had spent a long time in the States, was there and he dominated a lot of the conversation. He talked about when he had been in San Francisco. As Jack had also been in North America in the late '60s, there seemed to be some sort of rapport between them.

At one point, the Swedish-American exclaimed, "I went to a hooker's ball once!"

In reaction to this, for some reason, Jack became all worked up and blurted out back at him, "What is a hooker's ball?"

"Well, it's what happens each year at Halloween when all the prostitutes get dressed up and go out..."

"Wasn't there a big thing about it one year?"

Later, Jack explained to Hamish that he had been annoyed that the Swede, whom he had assumed to be American by his accent, had been dominating the conversation without explaining to people properly what he was talking about, something that Hamish had noticed Jack himself doing quite often. He said, "I knew what the hooker's ball was!"

Later that afternoon, a Chinese woman came in, who sang and played the guitar. Jack asked her to play and sing the song *Working Class Hero* by John Lennon. At this, she laughed and claimed that she had never worked in her life.

As the magazine was going to be folding up due to lack of funds, they were going to have a leaving party. When they all started talking about what they were going to wear, she said that she might come to the party not wearing anything except body paint.

The *Bär Fax* people also mentioned that a young Danish girl kept sending them nude photos of herself which she wanted them to publish in the magazine.

On the way out, Jack remarked on a picture on the wall of a woman who looked by the expression on her face like a severe depressive.

One of the Irish guys who worked on the magazine said, "It's an anti-alcohol poster!"

After they were out the door, Jack pissed behind a van and they shouted after him to watch out......

One night, in a bar called the Morgenrood, Hamish met some young women followers of Bagwhan Shree Rajneesh, in their typical red clothes, who were sitting at a table opposite him. They kept staring at him, but Hamish was not sure whether or not this may have been meant as an invitation for him to come back with them.

Shortly after that, one afternoon, while walking up the Wrangel Strasse towards Kottbusser Tor, Hamish and Jack met a young girl with very light-coloured, short hair along with her boy-friend who had jet-black hair which he wore in a punk hairstyle. After they had started talking, the girl kept putting her arms around Hamish and kissing him, at which her boy-friend seemed slightly perturbed but, on the other hand, he did not appear to be really *very* jealous – and **he** was the one that Hamish could not help noticing was **exceptionally** good-looking.

Another night, they met a strange-looking man, with whom Jack appeared to be acquainted, in a dark, eerily deserted street. They had a long conversation about some mystical subjects and kept talking about strange things. This weird character mentioned, along with much else, that he had "burned all his magical books". Whoever he was, he seemed to be very heavily into the occult.... and he looked the part as well, dressed in a black coat, with a long, black beard, in one of these very dimly lit streets near the Wall.....

Soon after this, Jack started threatening violence and, so, Hamish had to leave the small, run-down apartment which they shared.

The first few nights, he slept first in a cellar and then in an attic. It was very uncomfortable and cold but no-one bothered him. However, he could not go on like *that* forever.

One day, he suddenly remembered that his old friends Ulf and Gerda had moved into a squat, of which he knew, near Viktoria Park, Kreuzberg, not far from where he had been working that summer and round the corner from the gay cafe where, also that summer, he had met the street theatre group, who had claimed to be into the occult and who had placed an ashtray full of wood-shavings in front of that teenage couple, causing them to give them such a strange look, which Hamish had found so amusing looking on from behind. The house was owned by an older German Jew who had left it empty since the Second World War as a protest against the holocaust. The squatters had occupied the house and he seemed to be in no hurry to have them thrown out. Perhaps, thought Hamish, being a Jew, he may have been more likely to be sympathetic to these young, left-wing anarchists who were anti-establishment. In any case, it was unlikely that he would have been on the side of the German authorities.

Hamish rang the doorbell, was allowed in and was introduced to a young Scotsman from Glasgow named Jimmy Paterson. He asked for Ulf and Gerda and was told that they were not there at present but that they would be back later. In the meantime, he struck up a conversation with this young Glaswegian and got to know him a little bit.

He had a skinhead haircut, was cynical about hippies and was into punk-rock but, on the other hand, he seemed to be quite well-read. However, when they asked each other what books they had read, it turned out that they had not read the same books, except that, as he found out later, he and his girl-friend Jane had both read *Hunger* by Knut Hamsun.

Jimmy also said later that he had read a lot about other subjects, such as about politics and about the war. He mentioned several times that, during the last few years, he had been thinking of going and fighting somewhere, perhaps in Northern Ireland. Hamish saw that here was someone with whom he would have a disagreement about certain matters but he didn't want to start an argument.

Jimmy came from the opposite side of the sectarian divide from Hamish's Irish friend Patrick Christmas and he noticed that, any time Patrick came round, they both avoided certain subjects.

While Jimmy was probably from one of the rough parts of Glasgow, his girl-friend Jane from Manchester, on the other hand, had come from a middle-class background and her father was, of all things, a nuclear engineer.

They both cooked good vegetarian meals, which they had been trained to do in a restaurant where they had worked in Amsterdam. Jane could be seen around the house much of the time always reading different books and it was probably from her that Jimmy had got his interest in reading.

As well as reading a lot, Jane also had mystical leaning and once gave Hamish a Tarot reading using a pack of cards that she claimed were a printed edition of a famous pack which had been painted by a woman under the directions of Aleister Crowley.

They both had jobs at the British Army base in Spandau, preparing food and Hamish also met someone who claimed that, when he had been working there, his job had been to clear the rats from under the cell where the ex-Nazi Rudolf Hess was imprisoned.

When the British Army found out that Jimmy and Jane were living in a squatted house, they were both sacked from their jobs. As Jane was pregnant by this time, however, she found out that, in her case, the sacking had been illegal. Hamish accompanied her to a free legal advice centre at the other side of Kreuzberg. She was reinstated in her job but there was nothing that Jimmy could do, so he was dependent on *her*, at least for the time being, a situation which seemed to be frequently causing friction between them. They would have many heated arguments and, at such times, Hamish would disappear off to go and see Klaus from Aachen, a quiet guy who worked in a bookshop but who was nevertheless very friendly. He would still keep any letters which had arrived for Hamish in Patrick Christmas's old flat, into which he had moved after Patrick had left.

Patrick Christmas and his friend Sean Fitzgibbon had said that they had thought that Berlin would have come as more of a shock to Klaus than it had to them. Klaus went around in a suit and gave the impression of being very conservative.

After a few days, Jimmy accompanied Hamish to collect his belongings from Jack's old place. They stopped at a supermarket on the way back to buy some food and left Hamish's bags and sleeping-bag in the entrance. When a woman coming out of the supermarket saw the sleeping-bag, she shouted out, "Schweinereien!", as if it had been the crime of the century to come into the entrance of a supermarket with a sleeping-bag. Jimmy turned round and said, "What's she freakin' out about?" and then went on to say, "I think that these people just say exactly what they *think*!" Maybe so, thought Hamish, but with no thought whatsoever given as to whether all this rude and arrogant behaviour could hurt someone's feelings and perhaps even build up in such a way as to throw someone's state of mind off balance.....

After Hamish had been staying in the house for a short while, a Scotsman in his early thirties arrived wearing a kilt. He claimed to have hitch-hiked all the way from Glasgow to Berlin wearing his kilt. What seemed strange to Hamish at first was that he looked almost exactly like a schoolteacher he had had when he had been a patient in a psychiatric institution as a teenager. He was also well-built, wore his hair long behind his bald head and also wore a bushy beard and a kilt.

Hamish had tended to feel threatened by this man when he was younger as he had the image of him as some sort of alter-ego and someone who always thought that he knew everything better than everyone else. However, this Scotsman in his early to mid-thirties, whose name was Jimmy Lee, turned out to be an entirely different character.

He was interested in the arts and would rush around the city to visit one artistic event after another, but kept saying that he would often end up running out of places "in a nervous rush".

He had been thinking of taking part in one of these medical experiments where institutions pay volunteers to try out new drugs or even sometimes risky operations with the person's consent. However, he said that, once he was inside the place with all these people listening to this German doctor giving a speech, he suddenly took "a nervous rush" and ran out.

Oddly enough, he seemed very sure of himself at first, and, it was only after having known him for some time that one noticed that there was an underlying feeling of insecurity which lay beneath this mask of self-confidence. Being well-built, he had been proud of the fact the he was strong and able to work hard, but the situation of unemployment which was creeping in everywhere seemed to have begun to erode his self-confidence as the only job he could find was in some factory where the foreman apparently treated him in an insolent manner. He appeared to be very upset by this and kept asking Hamish if he would take a job if he was offered one. What he did not seem to understand was that Hamish would have taken almost any job at that moment as most of his present problems had stemmed from his having been forced into unemployment, not having money and being stuck in a city which was jarring his nerves and for which he now only had a very bad feeling inside. He was desperate to escape anywhere more quiet where there might be some prospects of work but had no money to leave the place.

Jimmy Lee was also well-read, well-travelled and seemed to have had quite a lot of experience of life. He had been in Laos in the middle of a revolution and had been in a bad bus crash in Yugoslavia, but it appeared that he still couldn't handle Berlin.

He kept saying that he had started to suffer from severe depression lately, had been feeling suicidal and had even tried to hang himself a few times while he was living there in the squat in Berlin where he was staying and which was just down the road from the squat where Hamish was staying with Jimmy Paterson and his girl-friend Jane. Jimmy Lee had a girl-friend who was also living in the same squat as him and he had apparently tried to talk to her about his depression – but she was over-weight and he said that, for that reason, he couldn't make love to her. He once said to Jimmy Paterson's girl-friend Jane, "I'm sorry, but I have to admit that I just can't make love to over-weight people. I hope that doesn't sound sexist!" She replied, "No, it doesn't!"

He also said something about having a complex about his mother and was apparently religious. He told Hamish, Jimmy Paterson, Jane and a few other people who were in the room that he had been to a church service when he had returned to Scotland on holiday and described it. This was totally unsolicited information as probably no-one was interested.

Sometimes, he would also bring out a Bible and start to read it whilst walking along the street on the way back from work. He said that he was starting to read the Bible because he hoped that it might help him to feel better but, then, after a few minutes, he would still start to go on again about how he was feeling so terribly depressed, lonely and suicidal and how he had again tried to hang himself the night before yet another time in the squatted house where he was living.

He also said that he was frightened to go back to Glasgow because he said that he would be alone in some house there where there were no work prospects. Hamish could sympathise with him on that score.

He said that, when he had been over to the East on a day visit, he had visited some of the churches there and told everyone that, whilst many people in the West were under the impression that religion was not allowed there, the people in the churches in the East had told him that this was not the case and that they were allowed to worship and to practise their religion in the same way as in the West. He also said that he "liked the streets" in the East and that he would rather there than in the West, in reaction to which Jimmy Paterson looked at him scornfully and exclaimed, "You must be joking!"

Another time, he told everyone in the squat that, when he had been in the U.S.A. before, he had "become a born-again Christian" but later went on to say that "it only lasted about half an hour".

He had been invited to "accept Jesus Christ into his heart" by a group of born-again Christians and had accepted it at first but had apparently, shortly afterwards, changed his mind and kept it to himself, as, when one of these Evangelists had called on the group to give a welcome to the Scotsman who had "accepted the Lord into his heart", he was too embarrassed to walk out but, after he had left, he never went back to see these people again.

Once, at a disco at the other end of Kreuzberg near the Wall, which Hamish had been to with some people now and again, where there were many outlandishly-dressed punks and what must have been the beginnings of techno music, Jimmy said, "This is no place for an old hippy like me. To me, this is the last thing before the Apocalypse......."

One day, Hamish, having discovered that, it being near Christmas, his Social Security money had not been paid into the bank in time, went round to the Berliner Volksbank with Jimmy Paterson and Jane to try to find out what had happened.

They asked him to sit down and wait for a while.

When Hamish saw what happened next, he could not believe his eyes.

The people working in the bank, led by the bank manager himself, all started dancing and clowning around and poking fun at him and all this was going on in front of his two friends who were also sitting there waiting. Jimmy was probably from one of the rough parts of Glasgow and put on a hard face, so what must he be thinking of him, apparently allowing himself to be made a fool of like that in such a way that he would never have dreamed possible until a few minutes ago (and he still couldn't believe it)?

It occurred to him that, if anyone had behaved like that in a bank anywhere except Berlin, they would all surely be sacked on the spot. He had never seen anything like it.

He had never before seen grown people behaving so much like children and could not believe how they could do such a thing and think that they were clever. It also reminded him of seeing old films showing the Nazis taunting the Jews at the start of the Third Reich. Had people really not changed since than? He had thought before that they had, but had he been mistaken?

This was much more than just embarrassing, it was very much more humiliating than anything he could ever have possibly imagined happening.....

And how had he allowed it to happen? Did he really look so stupid that grown people working in a bank of all places could make fun of him like that in front of his two friends that he shared a house with? Recently, something like this had been happening to him just about every week and he couldn't understand why. Was it "body language" as his friend Jack had suggested? He had no way of knowing for sure as he didn't see himself, so it triggered off a deep-seated psychological fear inside.

But then what could he do? He could not withdraw his account or threaten to withdraw his account as they were the only bank that the Social Security office would deal with, he needed the money and he could simply not find a job at the moment, in spite of having searched everywhere and if, for instance, he tried to smash the place up, they would call the police and get him into trouble or have him sent out of the country which would have been what they had wanted.

Hamish heard Jane say something sympathetic to his plight to Jimmy, to the effect that it was terrible the way they were treating him, but Jimmy just sat there and said nothing.

After the transactions were over, he walked down to the Underground station boiling with rage and that was when it all started to go wrong.....

On the train journey to where he was going, all sorts of insults and humiliations that he had had thrown at him in the past kept echoing through his head, such as, "You're just a middle class twit!", "Get out, or you'll be thrown out!", "Get out of here and don't ever come back again!" etc. etc. etc. etc. etc. etc. etc. etc. etc.
etcetera..

At the station at Kottbusser Tor, as it was starting to get dark, Hamish unexpectedly met the good-looking young punk whose girl-friend had taken a fancy to him.

The young punk said that he would be going out that night in a way that seemed to be an invitation to him to spend some time with his girl-friend as she apparently wanted to see him.

Normally, he would have been very pleased about this and, of course, with the conscious part of his mind he **was** pleased but, even after he had heard this, the anger inside him would still not subside.

All that he could think about was an extreme, uncontrollable feeling of rage burning inside him which would simply not leave him and which would need to be let out as soon as possible on anyone or anything......

For some perverse reason, he started to fantasise with part of his mind about being nasty to the girl and giving her the brush-off, somehow as if as a way of answering back to all the women who had given him the same treatment, such as the girl in Cologne who had shouted at him, "Get out of here and don't ever come back!", but he didn't really seriously think that he would be capable of behaving in such a bizarre and ridiculous manner and, besides, he liked the girl and wanted to be with her..... but then he was not thinking rationally and his mind had slipped temporarily out of control......

After he had reached the squatted house where the young couple lived and the girl's boy-friend had left, Hamish still felt all this rage boiling inside him from what had happened before that day in spite of his having been left alone with the girl. He asked her why she had invited him round there. She said that she felt a very strong compassion for him. He should have been obviously more alert and taken some comfort from what were her obviously sympathetic words but the sheer rage and frustration that had already been planted in his mind would still in no way leave him. He could control himself no longer. For some utterly perverse reason, which he probably did not even understand himself, he blurted out that that was her problem, not his problem, which seemed to be a peculiar Berlin expression that people had used to him before when they had been annoyed with him about something.

She then gave the impression of being upset and said that he was making her feel confused. If he had had any sense left, he would still have stayed with her and tried to talk to her and explain what had upset him so much that afternoon, to which she might have leant a sympathetic ear, but his mind just was still not functioning rationally at all and the boiling rage inside him had still not left him, so he shouted at her to stay away from him and went out and slammed the door as if he was defending himself against he knew not what and was making the last pathetic move in a chess game. He should have realised that what he really needed was a sister of mercy when he had thought that he just couldn't go on.

On the way to the Underground station, he seemed to feel some sort of perverse satisfaction in what he had just done, although he still felt all confused inside..... but then he had had to let it all out and he just couldn't help it.

He had gone the way fate had pointed him like a man walking in his sleep and, for once in his life, the dark side of his personality had completely taken over and he had not been strong enough to do anything about it..... but then there always comes a time when every careless word has to be answered for.....

Watch, therefore, for you know neither the day nor the hour.

Jimmy Lee came round that night to the squat where Hamish, Jimmy Paterson and Jane were living, literally shaking with nerves from head to foot and in a terrible state. He wanted someone to get a hold of some acid for him, which Jimmy Paterson tried to do, but was unable to because none was available at the time.

Jane asked Jimmy Paterson if he thought that Jimmy Lee should really take acid in the state of mind that he was in but Jimmy Paterson said that he thought that it was up to him and Jimmy Lee said that it might put a different perspective on things.

The next morning, Hamish was frightened to think about the previous day's events, which had upset him so much, and tried to push the memories of what had happened to the back of his mind. He went round to see his friend Jimmy Lee in the other squat where he lived in a rather wretched and freaked-out state of mind.

He found Jimmy Lee there in the upstairs room in the squat where he lived in a quite agitated state of mind himself. At first, he had quite a large stack of marijuana, which he proceeded to get through very quickly as he was smoking one joint after another although, on the other hand, he refused to take a drink of wine from a bottle which Hamish had bought and brought round with him, without giving any reason.

He then proceeded to roll and smoke one cigarette after another, which he rolled from hand-rolling tobacco, while, at the same time, pacing up and down all the time, not only up and down the room but also through a long corridor and out into a small kitchen and back through the same long corridor and into the bedroom again and again, always the same pacing up and down, back and forth and rolling and chain-smoking one cigarette after another all the time..... This went on for about one or two hours. During this time, at one point, Jimmy said to Hamish, giving him a sort of sly smile, "Come on, Hamish, give us a kiss!", which Hamish was unsure whether to take as a joke or not. In any case, Hamish left late that morning unaware of what was going to happen next.

When he went round there again the next day, he found several of the German squatters, including Jimmy's plump girl-friend, all looking very sullen. When Hamish asked where Jimmy was, she told him that he had hanged himself the previous day shortly after Hamish had left. She went on to say that, at the time, just before he had hanged himself, first that he had "no shoes on", which she later changed to "no clothes on" and also that he had been "acting strangely".

When Hamish arrived back at his own squat, a doll with a pin struck through it had been found there, which people said had been left there on the night before Jimmy Lee had committed suicide. Also, Jane later said that she was frightened even to go to the toilet at night because she felt that there was a creepy feeling in the house as if Jimmy's spirit was still haunting the place. Oddly enough, Hamish had exactly the same feeling.

Everyone was talking about Jimmy's death shortly afterwards as it had been reported on the front page of the newspapers the next day. When Hamish's Irish friend Patrick Christmas came round, he assumed that his death had had something either to do with his having taken acid or because he had been given tablets which had affected him strangely during some medical experiment. The odd thing about it was that he had not taken acid on the night he had come round for the simple reason that none had been available at the time and he had also not taken part in any medical experiment because of the simple fact that he had taken a "nervous rush" and had ran out of the place. Instead of that, now he was dead for other reasons which were probably unknown to all of them.

It was also during the following period that Hamish started experimenting again with acid, such as one night when there was a party going on in the squat where he, Jimmy Paterson and Jane lived and his Irish friends Patrick Christmas and Sean Fitzgibbon came round. He just didn't care any longer about any possible dangers to his mind, as his life was falling apart so much that nothing seemed to matter any more. Hamish played the piano in the cafe downstairs while the people in the squat listened and he later got drunk and took off all his clothes.

That night, Hamish had the most terrifying nightmare. He looked in the mirror and saw that he was going bald and that giant insects were tearing his hair out. He reached for some spray to kill off the insects and then woke up suddenly with a start in a state of fright. He wondered what all this could mean. Whatever it was, it gave him the creeps far more than anything he had ever known before in his life, by a very long way.....

The next night, he also had a very strange dream. He seemed to be working in a factory like where he had been working the previous summer, but, when he looked down at the conveyer-belt, instead of empty ice-cream cartons passing by, there were cheese sandwiches and, when he looked at them closely, he saw that they were in the shape of human skulls.

During one of his forays into town, Hamish met a rather eccentric German, while buying tobacco at a kiosk in the Bahnhof Zoo. This man, Manfred, fancied himself as a poet and an artist and went around trying to sell his poems and drawings in the streets with hardly any success while, on the other hand, spending a tremendous amount of money at a printers, for instance, and other places, but also on beer, as he was something of an alcoholic. He was getting all this money from his mother, who was a somewhat nervous woman, who seemed to be rather concerned about her son's behaviour.

However, Hamish was quite amused by Manfred's eccentricities. For instance, once, when hitching a lift, he ran out into the middle of the road to catch his hat, which had been blown off in the wind, which Hamish thought looked very funny at the time.

Hamish went around with him for a few days and they talked about all sorts of things but, everywhere they went, first they would have to drink a beer before they could do anything else, such as pay a visit to the printers or the newspaper office, to meet some friends or whatever else was on the agenda at the time, which usually included quite a busy schedule, as Manfred was very excitable.

One day, Manfred had the idea that, as a joke, that night they would go down to the red-light district wearing business suits, which had belonged to his father who was now dead, and go around telling everyone that they were businessmen.

This they proceeded to do and they both dressed up in suits, but, of course, on the way, first they would have to stop and have a beer somewhere.

They made their way to the bar at the Bahnhof Zoo. After a few beers, Hamish became a little excited and started singing, "Hey, Mr. Tambourine Man, play a song for me!" *

Of course, after that, they both became quite drunk and lost each other on the way. Later, Manfred said to Hamish that, when he had been looking for him that night, a girl whom they had met at the station had exclaimed, "Oh, was that the boy who was singing?!", as if she had been attracted to him......

The next thing that Hamish remembered after that was that he was woken up in the street by the police somewhere in the middle of the red-light district, having drunkenly slouched on to the pavement and fallen asleep. The next morning, he was embarrassed, finding himself walking around wearing a suit and having to ask all these young people for cigarettes, as he found that he was without any tobacco.

He was in an extreme state of exhaustion and needed to eat something and also to lie down somewhere as soon as possible, but he did not even have the strength or energy left to go home. He had just enough of the money left that Manfred had lent him to book into a youth hostel which happened to be nearby for one night and to order something cheap to eat.

He checked into the cash desk in a complete state of nerves and proceeded to the dining hall where they served very cheap food which was quite plain but, Hamish thought, very good food for the price and that it was what he needed at the time.

He was glad that he had had at least enough money left to find a cheap bed for the night and a meal and, after he had finished eating, he made his way to one of the bunk beds in the dormitory to lie down.

That was when the horrors all began.

He dreamed, at first, that he was in a building somewhere in Helsingør, Denmark, where Elsinore Castle is and from where the boats also leave to go to Sweden.

There were a lot of good-looking young people in this building who were holding an orgy and, at first, they all seemed to be very happy and having a good time.

However, after a while, for some reason, he started to get an uneasy feeling when he saw some crude pictures from pornographic magazines on the floor, which he found a little grotesque and off-putting, and also there was this creepy force which seemed to be telling him that he was either unable or not allowed, for some reason, to take part in this orgy. Then, it became apparent that this evil force was trying to propel him towards the back of the building for some reason, but he was frightened of it and tried to stay where he was.

In the end, this sinister force proved to be more powerful than Hamish and it dragged him somehow against his will to the back of the building and upstairs, where there was a door on the right-hand side, through which he was terrified to go.

Again, he tried with all his might to hold out against this force and to stay where he was, but, with all the will in the world, he found that he was unable any longer to hold out against it, the force proved stronger than him for a second time and propelled him behind this door to the place where he was most terrified to go and that was when he faced the ultimate horrors.

Having now been unwillingly forced behind this door, what he now saw before him gave him the final shudder.

Giant black phallic shapes started swirling round and round in circles in a way that seemed never-ending and he realised with an extremely intense shivering inside that he was now dead, that he was now literally in Hell and that this was now literally going to go on for ever and ever with absolutely no end for all eternity............. Or, at least, it seemed so terrifyingly vivid and real that he thought that this was the case.

He started to shout out, "Help!" in what he realised later was his sleep and managed to wake himself up after what he thought must have been a few minutes, but which may have been only a few seconds. He was lucky that he didn't have an 8-hour horror trip.

He woke up with an enormous sense of relief to get back to so-called reality and came to the conclusion that, even in this world with all its problems, at least the Devil-that-you-know is better than the Devil-that-you-don't-know. If this is what taking LSD does to people, he thought to himself, I just don't want to know about it. And he never took it again.

However, this diabolical sensation still lingered and never quite left him all day. In fact, it would still keep coming back to him to haunt him from time to time from then onwards.

For instance, when he walked down the street that morning, he remembered what two American G.I.s, whom he had met in a coffee shop in Amsterdam, had said to him about a law called S-1, which had existed under the Nazis and which they claimed had been reintroduced ostensibly to stop the Baader-Meinhof terrorists and, with the same surreal, cringing feeling inside, he realised that, if that was true, at least, in theory, the police could arrest him (or anyone, for that matter) at any time and take him away and keep him somewhere for as long as they wanted.

And then he imagined that they could be looking at him from every nook and cranny of every building as he walked down the street to the Underground station with that utterly, uncanny, eerie sensation which acid gives and which is almost impossible to describe.

Then he thought of what the Nazis had done to psychiatric patients in Germany before the war and a shudder went right through him......

He sat down on a concrete block outside the U-Bahn and started to think about everything. Somehow, now it all seemed to fit into place. As LSD seemed to him to be the most powerful thing on Earth at that time, the first human beings on Earth must have eaten from a hallucinogenic plant such as a cactus or a mushroom, which must have given them the knowledge of good and evil and they must have been expelled from Paradise for that reason. And, of course, that was when they had started to wear clothes, out of guilt..... and also why we *all* had to get back to the garden. And *quickly*. This was the last thing before the Apocalypse.....

One day, at about lunch-time, Hamish and Jimmy Paterson went to sell copies of *Bär Fax*, Berlin's only English-language magazine, which had been started up by Hamish's Irish friends, outside the University, as they had run out of money.

They were standing there for about two hours in the freezing cold.

They had smoked some hash before and Jimmy started to get the munchies. He went into a shop and bought a lot of chocolate and they both ate not one bar of chocolate or two bars of chocolate but at least three bars of chocolate.....

Then, they went to buy some chips, or "pomme-frites", from one of these Imbisses or stand-up food joints.

Next, they went to the Inter-Shop and bought two bottles of Polish vodka.

When they arrived back at the house, they finished off all the vodka and, needless to say, both of them spewed up in the toilet that night.

Another day, in the street, Hamish met his old friend Jack and they struck up a conversation. Amongst other things, Jack mentioned that he had seen the young girl again, who had the good-looking boy-friend with the punk hair-style, and said that she looked as if she was "in a very bad way with heroin".

This started to alarm Hamish and to reawaken some painful memories. He hoped that he hadn't upset that poor girl so much that she had started taking heroin because of his behaviour that night. Had she been a heroin addict before he had met her? He didn't know, but he didn't think so and had had no reason to believe it.

When he arrived home that night, he lay down on his bed and started to ponder on all things and particularly to reminisce on what had happened that awful night. People had been making a fool of him all his life, he still didn't know why and these people in the bank had made him look like a complete idiot in front of his friends.

Could it have been due to "body language" as Jack had suggested? Was he subconsciously giving out signals without noticing it? Was there something that other people all noticed about him that he didn't notice himself? As he didn't see himself, he had no way of telling but, since he had come to Berlin, something like that had been happening every week and it filled him with a deep-seated psychological fear and loathing.

It couldn't have come at a worse time as he was planning to leave Berlin soon and needed to keep that bank account open to receive his Social Security money, so that there had been nothing that he could have done about it and there had been no possible way of getting back at them.

He set his mind back to the time he had been in the house where that girl lived and he had asked her what she had wanted from him and then he had shouted at her when she had done nothing to deserve it.

At first, he almost felt quite chuffed that he had managed to get all this burning rage out of his system. He had, at long last, managed to get all his anger out. Or, had he really?

With a shock, he realised that he still hadn't got back at these people in the bank and, instead of that, he had taken it out on a poor young girl who had a nice personality and who had shown him some affection, who would probably have given him the love he required when he most needed it and who was the very last person he should have lost his temper with at that time.

And then he thought of her boy-friend as well, the good-looking youth with the punk hair-style, whom he had somehow liked and who had been kind enough to take him back to their squat to spend one evening with his girl-friend after he had met him at the Underground station at Kottbusser Tor. He had had a strong feeling of liking him and now he had probably also upset him. And he couldn't forgive himself for having upset both of them as they were two such nice people and he could probably have struck up some sort of relationship of friendship with them and they could all have given each other comfort when they just couldn't go on.....

Overwhelmed by a deep sensation of guilt in his heart, he felt as if he had committed the ultimate crime.

And then he started to imagine how the girl must have been feeling at the time that he had been in the house where she lived. She had seemed very sensitive and had perhaps looked upon Hamish as someone special in whom she would be able to confide and now, instead of that, she would always remember him as that horrible guy who had come in and shouted at her to stay away from him in a fit of temper and for no apparent reason.

And how could he have been so cruel to someone that he had had such a strong feeling of liking?

Suddenly, he burst into tears and the lines of an old song from the 1960s came back to him:

> "Someone left the cake out in the rain
> I don't think that I can take it
> 'Cause it took so long to bake it
> And I'll never have the recipe again....." **

With an almighty shudder, he realised that it was all over now and decided that, the next day, he would put an end to it all.

He had come to the last days at the end of everything when every careless word would have to be answered for......

Late the next afternoon, with a bottle of sleeping tablets in his pocket, which he had somehow manage to persuade the doctor to prescribe him, Hamish stood looking at bottles of alcohol for the last time in Uhland's liquor store opposite the Bahnhof Zoo.

He had never in his life seen such a varied selection of drinks from all over the world. There was wine from everywhere from Argentina to Czechoslovakia, there was Norwegian Aquavit, there was Yugoslavian Slivovitz, there were all sorts of things.....

In the end, his eyes landed on a bottle of Southern Comfort. As he paid for it at the till, the cashier didn't even look at him and obviously could have had no inkling as to what was going on in Hamish's mind or as to what he was going to do next. He put it in his bag and went out.

He made his way down into the U-Bahn and on to an Underground train for the last time in his life, returned to the squat where he lived and, after having swallowed all the sleeping tablets, sat down on his bed to have the last drink of his life. He thought that he might as well at least try to enjoy it as it might bring him a few final grains of comfort.

As he lapsed into unconsciousness, some words echoed through his mind which he seemed to have a vague recollection of having heard or read somewhere:

"You will never get out until you have paid the very last penny....."

Uden, The Netherlands
October 2000

*   words by Bob Dylan
**   from the song *MacArthur Park*, words by Jim Webb, originally recorded by Richard Harris in 1968

A Sixties Prodigy

Little Johnny grew up in the 1960s in a quiet backwater of a winding suburban street in a sleepy little town in the middle of Scotland.

There was a telegraph pole at the bottom of the back garden which somehow gave Johnny a weird feeling, there were several gardens behind that leading to houses that faced on to two other streets and, across the road at the front of the house, there was an overgrown path leading to a field where boys played at night.

His father worked in a bank and his parents were what Johnny would realise later were known as "lower middle class" people, without much imagination – but Johnny had a powerful imagination which would transport him into vast vistas in the nooks and crannies of his mind, of which his parents – and most other people – could only have caught the very merest glimpse.

Johnny shared a room with his older brother Dave, who was about 15, and, one day, when Dave was undressing, Johnny noticed with curiosity how well-developed he was. Their mother came in the room and Johnny secretly wondered if his mother had enjoyed seeing his brother undressing.

Johnny had, at one point in his early childhood, had a spate of nightmares, but had not been afflicted with quite so many bad dreams recently.

On the wardrobe in Johnny's and Dave's room was a strange-looking brass door-handle which was shaped like a pair of eyes at the top and came down to a point underneath. Johnny always felt as if it was looking at him, so, each night, he would undress quickly and rush into bed before the handle could catch him. He must have heard of the idea of reincarnation somewhere because he imagined in his mind, for some reason, that he must have committed suicide in a previous lifetime and that the last thing that he had touched before he had died had been the door handle, which must have been why it seemed so eerie and frightening. When he thought about this in later life, he had absolutely no idea how all this could have come into his head as a small child.

One day, Johnny's father took them through to Glasgow to do some shopping. Johnny had never seen slums before and was shocked by seeing what seemed to be never-ending rows of broken-down houses going on for miles with seemingly absolutely no ending. He noticed in passing from a street sign on a corner that one of the streets was called "Rottenrow" and he thought to himself that the name described just exactly what it all was, just rotten rows of houses.....

There was a house down the street where Johnny lived, which belonged to a woman whom the boy across the road would go and visit sometimes, referring to her as his "aunt". However, she wasn't really his aunt but a friend of his mother's. She was divorced from her husband and was living with another man and tended to be looked at slightly askance for that reason. Johnny's parents never really explained it to him properly, although his maternal grandmother did say to him once, "It's a difficult situation, you see!"

The man she was living with had a dark blue Audi car which he kept parked outside the front of the house all the time. His father said, "That chap's trying to do something like Mercedes Benz," but that remark was lost on Johnny who didn't realise that Audi was also a German make of car.

One night, Johnny had the most disturbing dream that this house was being taken down although there was nothing structurally wrong with it until, in the end, all that was left was a large pillar standing in the middle surrounded by a pile of rubble. When Johnny was older, he would be reminded of this dream on seeing pictures of cities that had been bombed out during the war, but he didn't recall having seen anything like that at such a young age – or, perhaps it had been the sight of all these broken-down houses in Glasgow.....

Of course, Johnny realised that some houses had to be knocked down if they were old and unsafe to live in, but nearly all the houses in that street, apart from a few older ones at the top end near the funeral parlour, were nice houses that had been built in the 1950s and there was something about the idea of houses being knocked down when there was nothing wrong with them that for some reason gave him a very uneasy, creepy feeling inside......

Another night, Johnny had a dream that he was travelling with some people in what seemed to be a small, old black car. They were enjoying the scenery when suddenly the car came to a halt at their destination which was an old, sinister-looking castle with two pillars on each side reaching up into dark turrets.

The castle was called "Klas Castle", with what Johnny noticed was a strange spelling.

There was something unreal and almost demonic about this castle, which was the final outpost of their journey in the middle of nowhere.

Of course, at that time, Johnny had never heard of prisoners being kept in castles during the war and it probably wouldn't even have occurred to him that the name "Klas" was spelt like a German name.

Johnny was always affected by music from a very early age. What must have been the first record he ever heard, at the age of three, of which he would later have only a very distant recollection, was Anthony Newley singing *Strawberry Fair*, which, he was later to learn, came from a stage musical called *Stop the World – I Want to Get off!*

The next year, as he would remember later, he heard Carole King singing *It Might as Well Rain Until September* and, oddly enough, Pete Seeger singing *Where Have All the Flowers Gone?* Although Johnny had no idea at that time what the song was about, one of his earliest memories was of his mother sitting writing out Christmas cards while that song was playing on the chart show on the radio and saying to him, "You know, Johnny, sometimes I feel very weary," but, on the other hand, she would never talk to him about herself or whatever it was that she felt weary about.

Other records which Johnny heard during the next couple of years were **Speedy Gonzales**, **Telstar** by The Tornados, **The Young Ones** by Cliff Richard, **Stranger on the Shore** by Acker Bilk, **Island of Dreams** by The Springfields, a number of records by The Shadows, The Cascades singing, "Listen to the rhythm of the falling rain...."* and, last but not least, the theme of the kids' Sci-Fi TV series **Fireball XL5**, which he went to see once a week with his brother Dave on a small black-and-white television set in a black case at their grandmother's small cottage on the outskirts of town underneath the main road to Glasgow, as their parents still didn't have TV at that time.

That was the song with the lyrics:

> "My heart will be a fireball
> And you will be my Venus of the stars......." **

You couldn't get much more romantic than that!

Like many children who had lived through the bitterly cold winter of 1962-63, Johnny had vivid memories of it for a very long time afterwards.

One day in May 1963, Johnny went into town with his mother and brother Dave to do some shopping and one image which would stand out in his mind was that, on the way back from town, the buses were so covered with snow that it was impossible to read the destinations on the signs in front of any of them and, thus, one could not tell where they were going. Johnny's brother Dave had bought some records. Their parents had one of these old-fashioned gramophones and some old '78 records of tunes like **Donnawellen**, **Over the Waves** and **Stars and Stripes Forever**. There was also an old classical record called **Serenade**, which neither Johnny nor Dave liked very much. However, Johnny had wanted to buy some of "these new type of records", meaning vinyl singles, which must have started coming out at that time.

Dave bought two records that day, one called **Polly Wolly Doodle All the Day**, with the actual plastic on the record pressed in bright colours, which must have been an early gimmick, and the other being **Summer Holiday** by Cliff Richard, which was one of the most popular songs at that time.

Later that year, Johnny would go with his mother and brother to see the film **Summer Holiday**, which Johnny would see once again many years later as an adult, but would remember very little about it from having seen it as a child, such as that there were some sexy-looking teenage girls in it or that they had driven through Yugoslavia to Greece in a double-decker bus, a journey which Johnny himself would make in later life (but not in a double-decker bus!) or that they had visited a "shotgun wedding" in Serbia and were shot at themselves on leaving. In any case, the bus did eventually pass through what at that time was the very southernmost tip of Yugoslavia – and which is now known as the Former Yugoslav Republic of Macedonia – without too many mishaps, although it did sway from side to side a bit before it reached Greece as if it had been driven by Dean Moriarty himself, the legendary hero of Jack Kerouac's cult novel **On the Road**, which, later, as a teenager, Johnny would learn, had apparently caused a stir in the U.S.A. in 1957, the year Johnny was born, and had led to the formation of the "beat generation" or "beatniks", who had gathered in the North Beach area of San Francisco in the late 1950s and early 1960s, out of which the flower-power movement would emerge and hit the media 10 years later in 1967 when Johnny was 10 years old and would hear everyone talking about "hippies" in San Francisco handing out flowers, preaching "love and peace" and practising "free love".

Johnny had also heard the term "beatniks" as a younger child but had no idea what it meant, nor did anyone probably.

Some time during 1963, Johnny and Dave heard The Beatles' records for the first time and the rest was history. Starting with **From Me to You** and then **Please Please Me**, which they actually heard later, either Johnny or Dave would buy each of The Beatles' records when they first came out and shot straight to No. 1 – and it was later, on hearing **Strawberry Fields Forever** when it came out early in 1967, along with the strange video that was shown on **Top of the Pops**, where they poured paint down the back of a piano in a park, that Johnny realised once and for all that music was definitely his main interest in life and that he was *not* interested in football.

In fact, try as hard as he could, Johnny just could not concentrate on hitting the ball for more than one or two seconds as his mind would always wander off somewhere else.

On the other hand, Johnny was very clever at school and would always be the first in the class at Arithmetic and later at Maths – and his mother would repeatedly relate to him throughout his life that a neighbour had once said to her over the fence in the back garden that "that child is going to grow up to be a genius" because he had learned to tell the time before he had gone to school and teachers would later say in the final year at Primary that Johnny would sometimes embarrass them in the Maths class by proving them wrong and telling them the correct answers.

As a small child, at one point, he became very fascinated by codes, had memorised all the street names in his home town from a map and had various I-Spy books, his favourite of which was **I-Spy – The Sky**, a simple book for children about astronomy, which he found the most fascinating subject of all – but his mother would look askance at him for taking such a keen interest in that subject.

His parents had also sent him to piano lessons as a small child but had stopped them later when they discovered that trying to keep in time with a metronome was getting on his nerves.....

Johnny's father very severely reprimanded him for masturbating, having been very strictly brought up himself in a small coastal town in the north of Scotland by his own mother who had belonged to a very puritanical religious sect, which appeared to be an off-shoot of the Plymouth Brethren, but which was known around there simply as "the Brethren".

Johnny never saw his paternal grandmother much, except once a year when they would all go on holiday to her house in his father's home town, where his two great-uncles also lived, one of whom stammered all the time and talked to himself.

She died in 1966 when Johnny was only nine years old so he never really got to know her, but he knew that she was very strict and wouldn't even allow them to go to the beach or to listen to **Pick of the Pops** on the radio on a Sunday – and she was also very strictly against alcohol, much to Johnny's parents' annoyance.

Johnny's paternal grandfather had died when Johnny's father had been only three years old and Johnny realised, only much later in life, that his father may have been jealous of him for being the only one in the family with brown eyes.

Every other weekend, Johnny's father would start a blazing row about something, Johnny would always be the victim and would end up bursting into tears and wishing that Elisa, his girl-friend from when he had been about 5 or 6 years old, was there.

When he was older, a Dutch friend, who smoked very much marijuana, asked Johnny to try to remember his father's exact words when he had told him not to masturbate but, try as hard as he could, Johnny just could not recall a thing. Nearly 10 years after that, it came back to Johnny that his father had kept shouting at him, "Will you please stop *doing* it!" and that, at another point, he had kept shouting at him, alternately, "You *can* horn!" and, "You *can't* horn!", a memory which Johnny later realised must have lingered in his mind until after he had been placed in a psychiatric unit at the age of 12, as he then also recalled having told his psychiatrist about it. At the time, Johnny had had no idea what his father had meant by "You *can* horn!" or by "You *can't* horn!" or why he kept switching alternately from one to the other, leaving Johnny utterly confused and bewildered.

Later, Johnny realised that he must have developed sexually at a very early age, of which his father may have been jealous, but, at that time, Johnny didn't even realise what it was that he was doing. In fact, he didn't learn the facts of life until the age of 12 from some other kids at the last year at Primary and first heard the word "masturbation" from his psychiatrist later that year after he had been placed in a psychiatric unit against his will on the 17th of August 1969. He would remain there for two and a half years until he was 15. He would later discover that he had been admitted on the third day of Woodstock festival – and one month after the Moon landings (when Neil Armstrong had made a giant leap for a ape and one small step for a Superman – or, was it the other way round?) – and that he had been released on the same day that 13 innocent, unarmed civilians had been shot dead by British troops in Northern Ireland on Bloody Sunday.

The psychiatrist had told Johnny that he had thought that there was something wrong with his mother, but he would never say that to her face – although, on the day of his release, he did say to Johnny privately, "Some patients here really have something wrong with themselves but, in cases like yours, it tends to be more of a *family* illness."

What many people still do not realise is that, at that time, it only took any one doctor and any one social worker to sign anyone away for life – and the doctor didn't even need to be a psychiatrist.

The families would often collaborate with the psychiatrists to keep one undesirable or, at least, "questionable" member of the family in there out of the way as was, only in the 1960s, brought to light by R.D. Laing in his books *Sanity and Madness in the Family* and *The Politics of Experience*, which Johnny would later read, and by hippy guru Ken Kesey in his 1962 novel *One Flew Over the Cuckoo's Nest*, which was, of course, made into the famous film of the same name in 1975.

It so happened that Johnny first heard of the book *One Flew Over the Cuckoo's Nest* at the age of 17, before the film was made, from Tom Wolfe's book *The Electric Kool-Aid Acid*

Test which, at that time, was considered amongst people in the scene to have been the definitive account of the start of the hippy movement in the U.S.A., and which had been recommended to him – along with Hermann Hesse's *Steppenwolf* – by someone in a hippy commune where Johnny had thought that he had "lost his virginity" to a sexy young girl called Rita, who was an art student from Birkenhead, until many years later when a strange memory deeply embedded in the very most distant recesses of his subconscious would eventually rise to the surface in a most intriguing was after having lain dormant for more than 35 years..........................

*   *   *

After Johnny's father had stopped him from masturbating at the age of 5 or 6, that only served to make the urge and the desire *very much stronger*. At the age of 8, having stopped masturbating altogether for several years, Johnny suddenly thought of a *different* way of doing it.   His parents had repeatedly told him not to touch his penis but they had said nothing about him pressing down hard with it against the bed so, in his childlike mind, he thought to himself that this must be all right.

So, about every two weeks, when he felt the need to release tension and found that he couldn't go on any longer, he would go into his parents' room and press down hard against the maroon-coloured quilt on his mother's bed, which felt nice and soft against his penis.

Having not yet learned the facts of life, the only thing with which he could associate it in his mind was firing a salvo from the barrel of a gun.

He would go into a long fantasy in his mind about chasing a girl on a scooter all over town with a gun, about to shoot her.

While swimming in the sea on holiday that summer, in his father's home town in the north of Scotland, he had an erection and also fantasised about shooting a girl.

There was always a sexy-looking teenage girl with a slim figure and long, black hair who would walk past the window in the mornings on the opposite side of the street from the room where his parents slept in his grandmother's house, but he was never quite sure whether or not it was the same teenage girl he had seen each time.

In class at school, he would sometimes get excited and shout out at girls, "I'd love to shoot *her*!" to the somewhat bemused consternation of some of the teachers.

There was one girl called Jane with a slim figure and long, black hair and another girl he liked called Sylvia with short, blond hair.

Sometimes, on the way into town to go shopping with his mother, they passed a shop which sold guns. There was a strange notice outside the shop, which attracted Johnny's attention and which said something about "killing power". Presumably, he realised later, they must have been selling guns for sport or for farmers to shoot animals but, in his childlike mind at that time, Johnny thought that they were actually selling guns so that people could kill people and a shudder went through him – and, yet, every two weeks or so, he would keep fantasising about shooting a girl while pressing down hard against the maroon-coloured quilt on his mother's bed. He had heard of a very powerful gun called a .22 rifle and he thought that, maybe when he was older, he would buy a gun like that from that shop and then kill a girl that way – but, then, on the other hand, he knew from his own inner feelings that it was wrong – and God and his parents would disapprove..... but, try as hard as he could, he just could not get the thought out of his mind.....

If only he could think of a way of shooting a girl without killing her, he thought to himself one weekend, then that would be a solution to his problem..... and, then after he had been thinking about this for a while, all of a sudden, out of the blue, a profound revelation came to him as if "from above" – or from outer space, or somewhere – and a beautiful image appeared before him.

Instinctively, he had just thought of a *different* way of shooting a girl.

He would press up to a girl with his penis in the same way as he had pressed up against his mother's quilt and, in paroxysms of delight, it would vibrate in multiple spasms against her body and all this stuff oozing out of him would spill out all over her thighs as if it were vibrating and emanating across the whole universe. "Of course," Johnny thought to himself, "That was the *best* way to shoot a girl!" and a surge of joy flowed all the way through him as he made up his mind that, on Monday at school, he would shoot Sylvia in this *new* way that he had thought of – and, in his mind at the time, that seemed to be the most wonderful thing imaginable in all the world as if the thought must have come down to him from God – or from somewhere up in the sky – or from who-knows-where.....

When Johnny saw Sylvia at school that Monday, he said to her: "Sylvia, everything's all right now! I've thought of a *different* way to shoot you!"

"Johnny, why do you keep saying that you want to *shoot* me?"

"No, I don't mean *that*! What I mean is, I'm going to shoot you – like *this*!" – and, with that, his face lit up all over with a look of the most innocent, childlike glee as, without even realising what it was that he was doing and with a feeling of almost infinite pleasure as if he had just glimpsed Paradise for the first time, he thrust his penis into her as hard as he could about eight times in one minute and semen spilled out all over his pants next to her body in the most delightful way.

After a couple of minutes, to Johnny's surprise and utter bewilderment, she suddenly pulled herself away from him looking a bit upset and confused and took herself off first to the toilet to talk to her friends about what had happened and then, after that, to see the teachers.

Later that afternoon, one of the woman teachers there told Johnny off and said to him, "What you just did was something very *bad* to Sylvia!" – although she went on to add, with what sounded like a tone of sheer astonishment in her voice, "I must admit that *you've* grown up very quickly! Many adults have never done what you've just done!"

They were both kept off school for a short time and the teachers tried to explain to Sylvia what had happened and that Johnny hadn't meant to upset her.

When Sylvia came back to school after a while, Johnny was surprised to see her again. He said to Elisa, the girl who sat in front of him in class and who had been his girl-friend when he had been about 5 years old, "I thought that I'd *killed* Sylvia that time!"

"No, of course, you didn't kill her!"

Everyone told Johnny after that to forget about what had happened and not to speak about it and, with that, the memories slid on a conveyor belt to the very depths of his mind where they would remain for over 35 years until one night in middle age when it would suddenly all come back to him bit by bit.......

Den Bosch, The Netherlands
September 2001

* words by Jean Claude Gunmoe
** words by Barry Gray, sung by Don Preston

The Lost Sleeping Tablet

Dave was pondering over a map of the former Yugoslavia when he landed on Zagreb, the capital of Croatia, which he had visited in the summer of 1977 at the age of 20 and had made friends with so many 17-year-olds who were still listening to '60s music.

Most of them had travelled to the West at some point and were very interested in what he had to say about other places he had been to, such as Amsterdam and Copenhagen.

Having known people who had been to this country before, he was only mildly surprised to learn that the locals were free to travel in and out of and all around Yugoslavia at will and felt it to be a country which seemed to be moving forward and whose young inhabitants exhibited what he perceived as a unique friendliness and a liveliness which was quite unlike anything he had ever known before.

He also found that many of them were interested in literature and the arts and it was there that he met his first real love, Elidija, a music student, who was one year younger than himself. Although it was only a one-night stand, that evening when they had made love in her friend's flat in one of the back streets of Zagreb would always stand out throughout his life as one of his most treasured memories – and he was also very glad that he had been able to satisfy her as she was a virgin at the time.

Dave then found himself transported to the summer of 1986, when he had visited Belgrade for the first time and had met a young art student somewhere in town. They had taken a look in the window of an art workshop where some local artists or students had seemingly hurriedly put an exhibition together and they both agreed that none of the exhibits were very good.

It was a roasting hot day and, when the young student reached the flat where he lived with his parents and sister, after a long walk in the scorching heat, he removed his shirt and shoes.

It was at this point that he introduced Dave to his sister, a good-looking girl with long, black hair and a slim figure, who knelt down in front of him, also in bare feet, and exclaimed, "Serbian girls are the best!"

The young art student, whose name Dave probably never learned, then explained that the room in which they were sitting was his and his sister's bedroom.

It did not seem to Dave all that surprising that, in a poor area of a country like Yugoslavia, a teenage brother and sister would be sharing the same room, which, he thought, must have also been the case in other countries, probably including Britain, in the past.

At that time, people were keen to emphasise that they were one country and, when Dave visited Sarajevo that same summer, he thought that it was the most beautiful and unusual city he had ever seen – and the last thing that would have occurred to him was that there would be a war there six years later. He was also disappointed that the spool for his camera had run out by this time so that he was unable to take any more photographs.

His spirit at this point moved back to the map again where someone or something was trying to tell him that, in the future, the young people in Zagreb and Belgrade would be reconciled, but did not explain how this would be done... but it was found necessary to heal the town of Split, where the Diocletian palace was falling down.....

*   *   *

Dave was presently transported to the back garden in Scotland where he had played as a child in the 1960s.

In later life, he would realise how lucky he had been to have heard all the music at that time, when it had first come out, as he considered that something special had happened then, which could only have occurred once in the whole of human history.

His mind moved on to when he was 12 years old, when he had had some very vivid and profound spiritual experiences, which people around him at that time had confused with mental illness.

His father had had him incarcerated in a psychiatric hospital, where he was to spend two and a half years, and Dave would never be able to forgive him for having destroyed him spiritually as well as having taken away two and a half years of his youth, which he would never get back and, due to which, he would never be able to form steady relationships, his courtship with a young girl there having been put a stop to by the hospital authorities.

Dave's mother, on the other hand, was convinced that Dave, who was always the first in the class at Maths at school, was going to be a genius, but his education was neglected in the hospital and he would never be able to make much of his life....

In fact, throughout his whole life, Dave's father had never been able to accept the fact that he had ever grown up and would continue to play psychological games with him. For instance, only a few years before, when Dave was in his forties, his father, having lured him back to his house to see whether or not a certain magazine had arrived for him in the post, had threatened to call the police because Dave had accidentally dropped a cup and saucer into the sink. This, in turn, brought back all the old traumas of what his father had done to him when he was younger, the memories of which he had been desperately trying to shake off.....

At this point in his spiritual journey, Dave flew into a blind rage against his father, who had died the previous year, having left his son with no further chance to let out his anger at him.

*　　*　　*

Dave now found himself again as a 12-year-old wandering down the garden path with some of the other children in the hospital, many of whom would walk around half-dressed or with no clothes on at night.

He had felt all his life that they were talented young people who had been misunderstood by society.

At this point, the image of a memory also flashed through his mind of a good-looking youth whom he had seen running naked into the sea in Denmark while at the beach with his family in the summer of 1976.....

In Dave's later teenage years, he had also identified himself to some extent with the hippy or alternative culture. It had seemed to him, on learning history at college, that the world had, in the past, been going through a very dark age, which had culminated in the rise of the Nazis and had resulted in the invention of the atomic bomb which, as a 16-year-old in the 1970s, he worried about being in danger of destroying the world.

It also seemed to him, however, that the heroes of the new culture were trying to exorcise the world of evil spirits and to herald in the possibility of the dawning of a new age and a bright new future.....

It was at this point that he met the cynical atheist Richard Dawkins who pointed out that the Nazis had had so much power and had managed to do so much evil through believing in something irrational, namely the occult, an opinion which the burly school-teacher, who had taught him in the mental hospital, would probably also have shared.

He also associated this with the irrationalism of "born-again Christians", one of whom had tried to brainwash Dave in his tent the year before when he had found himself homeless in

Amsterdam and had told him that his present sufferings had all been due to his sins of the past and that he must repent of having had sex outside marriage, something which Dave could never possibly accept.

Dave could also have counteracted Dawkins by replying that Stalin, who was also a cynical atheist, had been just as evil as Hitler, if not more so in some ways, but, for some reason, that argument escaped him at the time.

Dave was glad that he had been born at the time he had and that he had not had to live through the Second World War. He also noted that it was in 1957, the year that he was born, that Jack Kerouac's *On the Road* had been first published and that it was during that year that John Lennon and Paul McCartney had met each other in a park in Liverpool which, in his mind's eye, seemed to resemble the back garden where he had grown up in Scotland and also a park in Croxteth where a 10-year-old had been murdered a few days before.

Someone was talking about Lennon and McCartney meeting at the park in Liverpool in 1957 and also interjected that something strange had happened when they had met each other even earlier – in 1948.

Dave noted that that was shortly after the war, when there would still have been some sinister vibrations flying around and when the world was still going through a dark time.   He also noted that the two future Beatles must have only been 8-year-old kids at the time.

Whatever happened Dave never found out – as his spiritual journey was suddenly interrupted by the blood-curdling sound of the alarm coming from his mobile phone, telling him that it was now 7.30 in the morning....   And he would not be able to continue on his spiritual journey until he took the next sleeping tablet.............

.

The Last Thing Before The Apocalypse

The Saviours

The setting was apparently the inside of a building, which was lined with rotted wood and bore an inexplicable yet uncanny resemblance to an old barn; and up and down the length of this place, the walls of which I never saw, were laid long, wooden vessels which, as far as I remember, came to a point at one end; and they were something of the nature of church pews. On these "pews", making the most obnoxious groaning noises, lay every saviour that had lived and died in the history of the world: they must have been all of fifty feet long and they were thin: they all looked the same, each with his bald head, which only contained some black hair at the back, laid at the pointed end of the vessel; and there were also more vessels laid out at front for the saviours still to come.

Lying asleep, the opposite way round from the others, this time normal size, at the head of one of these "pews" meant for future saviours was a little boy, who would frequently catch my eye at many times and places. It seemed that he was imitating the saviours by doing this. However, my active brain thought up two other possibilities: the first being that he was dead and having close contact with the saviours; and the second being that he was still alive, but that, when he did die, he would be known as a saviour and occupy one of the "pews".

No less than three days after I saw this, the little boy gave a speech, every word of which I remember to this day:

"At the present moment, anyhow, I see no need for anger, nor for anything which causes people to be upset, or hurt, only need for love, for, in this way, we can improve our world and not have any of the things which cover up this fact, leading us towards missing the target altogether, for the way is one of coldness, softness, lightness, breezes, slow-motion, smoothness, grace, whiteness and cleanness. When we come to look at things as a whole, forgetting completely the things which bother us on this Earth, then we find that there is no need to worry steadily about anything at all.

"An animal, who – almost asleep amongst the most natural things on Earth – lives in his perfect world, with no worries nor interruptions of this beauty, calm, quiet, still and almost dead, and even when asleep still dreams of this lovely world, is truly living in absolute perfect peace. In order to keep in our minds that there is such peace in the world, we must forbid ourselves from doing anything obstreperous, trying to be the best kind of person, in a way that we see what really matters and what is an illusion.

"In this world, there are very many nothing people about whom we know nothing. They don't think anything about anybody, nor want to. Others lay down the law that they are right, scorning things that they don't like (or pretend they don't like) while the tones of their voices say that they are normal, which is not always true since they are grossly biased. But the best kind of person scorns nothing, does not try to be superior, and listens to what everybody, no matter who he is nor what he proposes, says. This person is a true friend, the best way to be.

"So my advice is to try to be this kind of person, try not to bark up the wrong tree and, if you have or have had an inferiority complex, remember that you are not inferior, but, at the same time, that it does more harm than good to try to be superior."

Peter G. Mackie

Journey to Greece

It happened one year that, after having gone through numerous conflicts with people and having lived in a number of frustrating situations, I started out on the holiday I had been planning for about the previous eight months. Looking back on that period of my life now, it seems to me that I was on to a good thing, but, nevertheless, there is no doubt that, at that time, I felt that I was finding certain emotional conflicts difficult to resolve.

The train slipped from Holland, through Belgium, Luxembourg, down through Strasbourg...

I was going to stop for the night in Basel, and, after asking whether the train was going there, came to know a young Austrian who was about sixteen years old.

When we arrived in Basel, we had to go through the customs from the French to the Swiss side. Probably because I was looking quite bedraggled after having been on the train so long, the customs officer eyed me suspiciously, looked up my name in one book after another, and, eventually, after having kept me waiting for about ten minutes, let me go with a dirty look. My friend, having looked back to see what was happening, asked me what was the problem. We spent the night in a youth hostel and I already began to feel that I was starting to escape the clutches of my recent confusion... at least for some time...

As my friend was going to Venice, the next day we took the train, which sped through the snow-clad Swiss mountains past lakes, while my friend talked about a book he was reading about primitive societies and how he would have liked to have gone swimming in the lakes. Coming towards Milan, he mentioned to me that he was frightened to speak German because of some trouble there had been there the previous year. Presently, we found a park to sleep in, where we spent the night. I had grown to like this young man and felt like putting my arms around him and cuddling him when he was

49

asleep but refrained from doing so as I wasn't sure what his reactions would be.

We were woken up by a shout. At first, I thought that it might be a robber, but it turned out to be a Canadian tourist who seemed to want company. The next day, we cooked a meal in the park, had a few drinks and spent the rest of the day looking for some church where there was a painting by Leonardo da Vinci, which we never found, before rolling on towards Venice…

We booked into the youth hostel, bought several bottles of wine and, later, my Austrian friend and I walked around a poor quarter, where a dog barked at us and my friend talked to me about how amazing the place seemed to him and how he'd like to be there with "some special girl".

As I'd planned beforehand to go to Yugoslavia to see some friends, I parted from both my new friends after about a week and made the journey alone towards Trieste. On the way, I had a conversation with an Italian woman dressed in black who looked like a nun.

When I arrived in Trieste, some young girls told me that I shouldn't sleep on a certain part of the beach as there was a military installation near there. I remember vaguely spending a bad night on the beach and sitting in the morning in the railway station cafe drinking a cup of coffee and talking to two young German boys who were going to Belgrade.

I arrived that evening in Koper, the first town across the border.

The effect of arriving there turned out for me to be a complete transformation of my feelings.

Outside the station, I showed some young people, who happened to be standing around, the address of a friend I had met the year before and enquired of its whereabouts. They were uncertain to begin with, but one of them bought me a pizza and a beer and, later that afternoon, introduced me to someone who knew my friend and who took me to the address. His sister appeared and told us that he wasn't there, so I resolved to leave the next day.

My new acquaintances introduced me to a group of their friends and we spent a fine evening drinking and talking and standing around in a park where a joint was passed around and someone made fun of some Italian tourists before I retired for the night with one of my new friends.

I remember the way I felt very relaxed that night.

*   *   *

The train rolled into Athens early in the morning, after we had spent twenty-five hours looking out the window at peasants and gypsies. For some reason, the song **Morning Has Broken** by Cat Stevens echoed through my mind as we walked through the sunlit streets in this new country at the farthest edge of Europe, which had been the destination for all of us.

We booked into a back room and I hung up some washing on the sunny roof, which dried in about half an hour.

I resolved to stay in Athens only a few days, after which I would head for Corfu. During this time, I had some fun with two young Danish guys, one of whom got drunk in the plaka, which I had to explain at the police station. It was all quite amusing, really.

*   *   *

I sat in the station cafe and, for some reason, was struck by people selling sweets and plastic bottles of orange juice, which somehow made it look like a toy station. I had always wondered what Greece would look like compared to other countries.

On the train that night, I asked a young girl with long, black hair the way to where I was going. So you could actually talk to a young girl in Greece!

I met some young people in the port of Patras, which somehow gave the impression of a dream I had had in early adolescence about crossing a river and not reaching the other side. I thought that I might as well get to know these people, so I asked them if they were taking the same boat. I had noticed that one of them was wearing a T-shirt bearing the words "Proud to be Swedish" so assumed that they were from Sweden. They were very youthful and seemed glad to talk to me.

I don't remember anything at all about the boat journey, but only recall that we slept for most of the night in a park somewhere - which must have been either Patras or Corfu town – and were woken up by the police soon after dawn.

Anyhow, I clearly remember when we waited in the bus station the morning after we arrived in Corfu for the bus to Paleokastritsa and, especially, the bright sun, and asking one of them to explain the name "V-Tyskland" on his money calculator.   (It turned out that "V-Tyskland" meant "West Germany").

I wondered how we could ever find the right bus with the Greek names.

We booked into a campsite near the beach and spent most of the mornings having breakfast at a café, most of the days lying on the beach and swimming, and most of the evenings drinking wine at the campsite and listening to tapes of Simon and Garfunkel's soundtrack to **The Graduate**, Abba and Elvis Costello singing, "I don't want to go to Chelsea". This went on for a few nights.

It so happened that, one morning, we were all sitting around in a café having breakfast and I was in quite a jovial mood. One of the girls clicked on to my sense of humour, someone said, "She likes you!" and that was how it started.

I didn't have much chance to talk to her over the next few days but, during the afternoons, I noticed her lying on the beach, with her long, dark hair, in a skimpy green bikini, the bottom half of which was tied around her thighs, and I realised that she was one of the most beautiful young girls I had ever seen.

Unfortunately, I found it too hot to lie on the beach in the afternoons, so I had to lie in the shade. However, I resolved to talk to her as soon as the opportunity arose. She appeared at this point to be having various casual relationships with her friends, which seemed to end every few days. I thought that it might be my turn some time.

It happened on about the third or fourth or fifth night that we were all sitting around drinking wine as usual, when I started to become quite drunk. We ended up sitting around in a café having a meal and drinking some wine. As I have said, at this time, I still had many unresolved conflicts within myself and still had the very unfortunate youthful feeling that the world was against me. A girl, who was a friend of the one I felt that I had fallen in love with, and who spoke English with an upper-class accent, said something which intensely annoyed me, after which one of the young boys – the only one of whom I noticed tended to have an aggressive expression on his face – started talking about how he didn't like immigrant workers in Sweden. At this, I exploded and somehow my unresolved paranoia erupted over my emotions of love for the girl.

The sky had become dark and the whole atmosphere charged with emotion and tension of the darkness and the strange landscape coupled with my intense feelings of anger as well as love for the girl instantly made something click within me and brought me back abruptly for the first time in a number of years to many experiences in my childhood and early adolescence, when everything was still awake and alive and stirring within my soul, but also tinged with anger, before I had blocked the doors on emotions and love and ecstasy, and so very much more... this also seemed to heighten my desire for rebellion... and gave me to realise that there was something deep within me which should have been resolved long ago...

In the end, I managed to let my feelings of love for this girl win over the conflict in my mind and resolved to go with them to the disco, where I had thought that I might have a chance to talk to her. We walked for several miles along the dark road. As we came near the place, a man, who seemed to know the girl, stopped to give us a lift. She said, "I see that you remembered about my foot". As we left the car, we met an American girl who started talking to her, describing how some man had acted in a deprecating way towards her when she was buying cigarettes somewhere. This conversation struck a chord with me, showing that many people must have had similar feelings to those I had that evening.

When we arrived, my first impulse was to make for the bar and order a drink, as I was unsure what to do next or when I would get a chance to speak to this girl. On returning from the bar, I lost them and, when I couldn't find them anywhere, I asked some English people whom I had seen speaking to them if they had seen these Swedish people who were my friends. They told me where to look for them. I found them and sat down to try to relax and have a drink with them.

I stared out of the window most of the time and noticed two lovers on the rocks near the sea. The music changed and I realised that I could ask her to dance, but somehow couldn't bring myself to speak to her at all...

Too late, I realised that my own aggression and nervous tension had spoiled what could have been the most beautiful experience imaginable...

The Singing Summer

It was coming on towards summer when the young, 18-year-old wanderer Mervyn Williams arrived at the agricultural camp in Cambridgeshire.

As his friend Will was already there, he made off to see him first. He was sitting around with some youths, talking.

Presently, he went to the office of the travel agent, who was a friend of his, to pay his accommodation, which he could barely afford. Luckily, he was given one of the better-paid jobs on Saturday and was paid at the end of the day.

As he was taking his luggage, all of which was contained inside a sleeping-bag, along to the locker in the dormitory, he met a young poet in a purple cord suit, two years younger than himself, who was also into Pink Floyd and who started to speak to him with a strikingly original sense of humour. "He is going to be a good friend of mine," he thought.

Meanwhile, two Italians came in and talked loudly in an extravert manner, as if they were trying to make a fool of everyone, which put Mervyn off.

It was rumoured that there were to be four hundred people arriving that weekend, many of whom would be foreigners.

Mervyn was glad that he had made this friend as he had been feeling disillusioned before, such as one feels on a rainy day, or even a sunny day, in a state of solitary loneliness. And so it goes on.

As his new friend had wandered off meantime, Mervyn felt that he should take a walk around, have a look at things and possibly speak to one or two people.

When he sat down on a seat near the front gate, a middle-aged rough character, with an aggressive look on his face, came, sat down and started talking to a youth who was sitting there. He talked very cynically about how "you young people have nothing to talk about. Why can't you talk about women or beer or something?" The youth replied in a slightly nervous, faltering manner, although being careful not to lose face.

As they were talking about drinking, Mervyn thought that he would ask where the bar was since it would soon be opening-time, there was nothing else to do and he was in that frame of mind anyway. He did not have much money, but could ask Will for some of the money he owed back from when he used to keep him instead of having him wandering the streets at night. Unfortunately, however, the latter did not have much money either, but was good friends with the travel agent, and could spare £1.

As he sat there in the bar, he thought of the absurdity of everything, the beauty of the young girls, the summer and the general scene around him.

After having sat for a long time alone, as it was yet early, Will came in and paid him, followed by his new friend Gerald, whom he had thought had disappeared. He was glad to see him back and began talking to him in a heart-to-heart manner.

He spoke also to the barman, who was a very friendly man. It was later discovered that he was an alcoholic. He was going to like it there.

Next day was Sunday. Mervyn and Gerald had previously decided that they would be up early to walk into the nearby town. It was a bright, singing happy morning, Gerald had changed into shorts and they talked of their past lives and loves, while all the land around seemed to answer, "Yes" to these two beautiful teenagers, wandering restlessly through life and appreciating all the voluptuous universe around them.

"What's this about you supposed to be a poet?" asked Gerald. Will had described him as "The Mad Poet" as he had known him in his earlier days. Gerald started explaining about how he liked to write short stories. There was a good communication between them.

Wandering with restless energy, they told each other stories, one of which was about Gerald making love to a girl in a haystack.

To be amongst all these young people was going to be like travelling to a Babylon of Light, a jewelled city of youth in a Golden Age.

As they arrived in Wisbech, they tried the door of the first pub, which was closed. They were great friends at this point, which is one of the most beautiful things to have.

As they talked and drank in the pub on the way back, they poured out their souls to each other in this quintessence of morning, a phenomenon which they would repeat, or try to repeat, to girls that night.

When they got nearer the camp, Gerald asked Mervyn if he thought that it would be worth running across some fields to get back there quicker, then went on to say, "Well, if you run across these fields, you'll get shot at, and, if you get shot at, you'll end up dead…so…"

An American girl named Sue was interested in Mervyn's poetry, and there was also a Norwegian girl. They had both been to Israel together. They talked for some time in the bar that night.

After the bar closed, there was a parade of drunken gypsies and lovers making for the snack bar. The sound of people vibrated against the blackness of the night, and, while they were waiting to be served, the Norwegian girl, who was by now quite merry, stroked Mervyn's arm. He stood there trembling with Dionysic excitement, staring into the vastness.

*   *   *

Next wonderful vagabond morning, they were up and out and working in the fields, after having eaten in the wooden hut.

They were given sandwiches to take for lunch and stood at the front gate waiting for the trucks to come from the nearby farms.

That morning, Mervyn and Gerald were working in an onion field along with a very loud, eccentric woman, who could easily have been regarded as a witch.

Since Mervyn was unused to hard physical work, his legs and back ached, and, when Gerald and he reached the ends of the rows, always before everyone else, he found some difficulty in sitting down. He longed for the evening when he could relax and drink, and he found that, in his head, was the image of a poem about a medieval peasant who finishes work, becomes drunk with a friend on a barrel of cider, and sits there all evening staring at the starry sky and the general scene of lovers walking hand in hand, drunks coming out of the inns and the noise of the evening.

At night, when the tired bodies finally arrived back for the evening, first they had their tea, which left an hour before the bar opened, during which time Mervyn wrote a humorous story about two solitary eccentrics living in the country.

There is nothing like the summer when everyone comes to life, and this particular summer was full of the aforesaid's voluptuous presence.

That evening, in the bar, they talked to two girls, one of whom was Irish. They left shortly, but would be seen again later.

While Mervyn was waiting for the time when he had arranged to meet the Irish girl at the front gate the next morning, he succeeded in writing the poem about the medieval peasant. Luckily, they were put on the same job, but it seemed unlikely to Mervyn that anything would come of it. They continued on their way, picking gooseberries, which proved to be a tedious business, not to mention most badly paid.

That night, they met the American girl again with one of her friends. After Gerald had left, she started to talk to him. "Will was telling me that you write poetry." She said that, since he wrote poetry, she realised that there must be something in him. They talked for some time about how they felt about everything.

After the bar had closed, Mervyn suggested that they go for a walk. As it was very cold, both he and the girl, whose name was Sue, went to put on some clothes. He went very quickly and, when he came back, he was restless with anticipation waiting for her by the post.

For a time, he thought that she might not come, but she arrived at last.

They walked together, through the huts, towards the field behind the camp, past the bleating noises of a night of lively debauchery. The stars were out, and she talked about how the sky in Israel was so studded with stars. Trees were swaying in the breeze behind this haven of summer delight.

When Mervyn arrived back at his hut that night, he wrote a poem about it.

Each night, the names were posted up, stating who would be put on which job the next day. Mervyn and Sue would meet there each night, or in the bar.

They had a lot to talk about. Mervyn played the piano, while she played the guitar and they both took part in the twice-weekly competitions in the club.

Each day would be the same hard slog, however, and, sometimes, this made Mervyn feel almost ill. This, combined with his temperamental nature and lack of self-confidence, plus the insensitivity of other people, was almost strangling him. Often he would sit down in the fields during the day, feeling too tired to work, and he never made much money, being human and drunken, and his boots were beginning to fall to bits.

*   *   *

There were lots of interesting people at the camp. There was a Norwegian who spoke English badly; two young Austrians to whom he could relate quite well; several lively Norwegian girls etc.

In Mervyn and Gerald's dormitory, there was the French writer Jean-Paul, who was interested in parapsychology and another Frenchman by the name of Pierre. This was originally. People came and went like eccentric, wonderful, roaming ants. It was all very exciting.

Later, there came a young organist who was interested in Mervyn's plays and short novel. This discussion came into being after Mervyn had received a letter from an actor-friend, who had tried to stage one of his plays the year before.

One night, when Mervyn, in high spirits, leapt out of the bar to speak to Pierre, as he passed by two strange people, foreign by their accents, one, who turned out to be a Norwegian girl, laughed and shouted after him, "Crazy boy!" He would frequently chase after this girl from then on, but, although she was also eccentric and seemed to be a female version of himself, she was full of the usual insincerity of young girls.

All this happened during this ecstatic summer.

*   *   *

Meanwhile, he continued his walks with Sue at night. He started trying to explain to her about how he tended to feel persecuted by everyone, a phenomenon which had resulted in his loneliness and isolation, but she, in her naiveté, seemed to think that it was merely due to the fact that he went around looking untidy, or the clothes he wore. He knew that she would never understand. No-one ever did, except for one or two spiritually aware eccentrics, who were in a similar predicament themselves.

And, like everyone else, she eventually left, along with her friends. He was very sorry to see her go, and wrote a letter to her the next day, which he posted from Wisbech. She was apparently going to a farm in the north of Scotland.

*   *   *

Now summer was drawing to a close. He spoke to the Irish girl Siobhan about leaving. He ranted on in his usual sarcastic manner about everything, the awareness of which generally put everyone off. And it was not possible merely to talk about the weather and pretend that everything was nice.

So he left one morning with two girls, friends of hers. He had already secured himself a room in King's Lynn. That morning, when he left, tears were trying to flow, as he left this girl to travel the long, lonesome, uncertain path to his destiny.

The Search for Love

It was unfortunate that Michael was put into a mental hospital by his parents as a teenager and that he had lost contact with the natural flow of life for which he had always hoped and yearned and for which he was going to hope and yearn for a long time. There were certainly advantages to being in hospital, such as being amongst other young people to whom he could relate. However, he always hoped to get out. At night, he would sit and play the piano, thinking deeply about this matter and pleasing people with his music.

He longed to leave the hospital and have relationships with girls. He had already had a relationship with one girl in the hospital, which the hospital staff had tried to put a stop to, and they also stopped Michael and another girl form merely being together in a room. During the period of time after his relationship with Diana, he spent many lonely nights brooding in great pain.

He was out. It had been decided between the head teacher and his psychoanalyst that he was to attend a technical college for a one-year course in office work. It was during one morning in school, when Michael was writing out the music that he had written for the piano, that this decision was made. Knowing this, his heart leapt inside him as he walked down the country road to the nearby small town to catch a bus home in the twilit night; thinking of the future. But where was the future? The future, in his head, was of swimming with beautiful girls in the sea and of making love to the same beautiful girls in the natural, caressing night.

*   *   *

But he was in for a shock. When he arrived at the technical college, it turned out to be full of hoodlums and rough sorts, the girls laughed at him and he was hardly ever even left in peace. He longed to go away... When he was 16, he would leave the whole scene to be part of something totally different... He would at least find some peace away from his parents and people who bothered him, if not a girl that he could love…

When he arrived in London, the bright lights and crowds of people mesmerised him. There seemed to be more different sorts of people and it was certainly more exciting than a small village in Scotland to Michael at that time.

At the hostel where he stayed, there were all sorts of people talking to one another late into the night. It seemed interesting. One man even offered him a job counting chickens in a factory, which he wouldn't do because of his vegetarian principles. And, besides, he was only there for three days. But, in the back of his mind, he thought that he would return soon.

Several weeks later, Michael saw, in a magazine that he had bought in London, an advertisement for a naturist club in Kent. On seeing this, he immediately wrote a letter there, to which there arrived a prompt reply. Michael worked out that he could live there very cheaply.

*   *   *

One day, Michael asked his father for £5, persuading him that he was going to buy some clothes. Instead, he took the cheap bus to London that night. As he boarded the bus, he was filled with excitement and fear. He listened to the conversations of the other passengers, which would always stand out in his mind, and, although he did not have very much money with him, when the bus stopped on the way down, he bought a cup of tea to calm his nerves.

The next day, the sun was shining when he telephoned his parents, shaking, and persuaded them that he needed a certain amount of money to survive. He kept walking back and fore to the post office where he expected to receive the Telegraphic Money Order, which he spent later that evening on joining the naturist club. As the train to Kent was leaving Victoria Station, the sun was still shining, there were crowds of people, as there always are in stations in London, and Michael felt a thirst such as he had never felt before.

*   *   *

With the help of what was left of his parents' money and a social security cheque, which he had forgotten about and found in his pocket, Michael managed to survive. To begin with, he would only eat bread and spent most of the time lying down trying to forget his hunger or reading Arthur Rimbaud's poems.

His best friend there had also been in a mental hospital and had a strange interest in black magic, and, with the help of a friend of another friend, he managed to obtain employment with a free newspaper in London, and, after several more weeks, was able to stay with a friend in London.

Meanwhile, he was able to be accepted by a small circle of people. He had joined a club, which tended to attract lonely people, where he became good friends with someone from Canada, who was quite an amazing character in his way and who had served some time with a religious organisation, as well as making several other acquaintances. He even occasionally drank – something which he had never done before – but this was only done in order to remain on the best possible terms with his small circle of friends.

*   *   *

In the newsletter of a voluntary organisation, Michael read a short article about a community of people, giving their address. Michael wrote to them, as he was in the habit of doing when anything interested him. To his surprise, a reply came almost immediately, inviting him round one evening.

He cautiously manoeuvred his body nearer the door. He wondered what he had let himself in for... Sitting around an open fire were several people, mostly young, along with an older Irishman who was talking with some vigour. There was a lot of talk about new ways of life and ideas which, at that time, very much attracted Michael. Later that night, he went home, having asked to join the community, mesmerised by the enthusiasm of this said Irishman, the smell of incense and the effects of the joints of marijuana which had been passed round. Coupled with this, there was an invitation for Michael to go with them to Speakers' Corner that Sunday to read his poetry. They went on the Underground, carrying a chair, on which the Irishman and his accomplice stood at the aforesaid Corner to make themselves noticeable. Michael moved his luggage round to the community the next Friday.

However, he soon came to see through what was going on. The Irishman, although partly sincere, seemed, with his friend, who echoed all his opinions, to want to make all the major decisions. Their experience of speaking enabled them to dominate the other members, all of whom, including Michael, eventually became fed up with it and left. Michael was now sure that he wanted to live in a room on his own, where he could quietly be away from people when he wanted. Luckily, he was able to find one on the same day that he left.

*   *   *

Now came Michael's second period of starvation. He had started a new job – a clerical job at the University – which was paid monthly. He, like the other members of the community, had poured all his money into it and they had yet to work out how much they owed him. It turned out that he received less than the amount which, by rights, he should have been given. He received the £80 which he had given the community on the night he joined, but not the money which he had given them out of his wages each week. And this £80 was soon to go. He lost his job, and, what with everything that had happened, was too paranoid to look for another one or to go to the Labour Exchange to register and to sign on. And, besides, he wanted and needed some time on his own. He spent a month out of work, wandering around Tooting Bec Common, which was near where he lived, drinking and thinking, and listening to music.

After this, he lived by doing temporary work on and off – at first, clerical and messenger work, then washing up in staff canteens, until eventually he registered with a temporary work agency dealing with industrial work. His jobs included working in warehouses and factories – making electric irons and loudspeakers – and messenger work.

By this time, it was early autumn. The Irishman had made himself notorious during the summer, his name was all over the papers, he had lost what he had thought to be his only real friend through an argument, and he began to sink into a general binge of disillusionment.

One night, after having taken a walk round the Common, he went into several pubs and drank five or six pints of cider, which was more than he was normally used to drinking. The experience was nothing compared to the ecstasies he had known at puberty, but it was very pleasurable and did offer glimpses of what he had known in the past. After a few nights, he decided to repeat the experience, and, very soon, his room was filled with bottles of cheap wine and cider and he drank in the local pubs every night. One night, he went to a party at a place where he had been before, where they were giving away free drink, having already downed two bottles of wine that day, and, when he woke up the next morning, he drank almost a whole bottle of wine which had been left over from the day before.

However, he spent most of the time on his own. For three months, he came home from work, where he hardly spoke to anyone, and spent long evenings on his own, drinking. It was at this time that he started to write the story he had been meaning to write for a long time... about his time in the psychiatric hospital, for which he had a deep feeling of nostalgia. One night, he came in completely intoxicated and, in a state of excitement, wrote twenty pages of his saga.

For a long time afterwards, he did not show this to anyone or even mention that he had written it and, even when he did start letting people read it, it was only to a few of his closest friends that he thought he could trust. One of them was amazed by it.

It was also during this period of time that he made up his mind that he would spend some time in another country the next year to see what it was like. He booked a ticket to Amsterdam from a travel agency dealing in cheap fares and carried it around with him wherever he went, as he thought that, in the state of disorganisation into which he had fallen – his room was always untidy – he would forget to take it with him.

He sat in pubs at night, dreaming of the future...

He had packed all his important things into one case, which he left behind with his friend who was a social worker in a children's home. All that he needed with him he carried inside his sleeping-bag (which was all he had, in which to carry it) and the rest he left behind in his room, which he had not even told his landlady he was intending to leave. In fact, he only made a definite decision to leave on the day that he left.

A woman who helped run the club to which he belonged had made arrangements for him to go to an agricultural camp for a spell – which depended on what would happen. When he went to deliver the case, the teenagers in the home reminded him of being in hospital.

On the day that he left, he discovered in his room a book of poems which he had forgotten to include in the case, so he had to post them on to his friend.

The train moved off. When he changed at Cambridge and boarded another train, it was so crowded that he had to stand... and it was hot... and his luggage was heavy...

When she started talking, Michael knew that she was a woman without a mask, such as he had been looking for... such, in fact, was the reason that he kept going round every night to his friend's flat where were always gathered a number of people to whom he could relate in some way. But never before had he met a woman who was sincere, who did not hide behind something, who said what she felt about everything... and who was actually interested in *him*. She asked him if he wrote poetry, as she said that he looked as though he would. He brought out some notebooks of his poems from the cupboard, and also later his story about the psychiatric hospital.

Presently, several of them went out for a drink. When they came back and she was about to go, she said, "I'll come round some time to read the rest of your story."

One evening, about two weeks later, she telephoned his friend's flat, asking for him. They went out to see a film. There was something really beautiful about that night. The flower of love was in bloom.

Several evenings later, she phoned up again.. and then again... and, then, she lost control of herself one night, pulled him towards her and showered him with kisses.

They would lie on the couch together for hours, lovingly caressing one another. She took a delight in tickling him and he loved it. And, one night, she told him that she wanted to make love to him.

They spent the whole beautiful summer together. They were not together all the time, as they both liked to be on their own for some of the time, but this was an ecstasy like nothing that had ever happened to him before. She was really bringing the life back into him.

He had had the desire to travel since the year before. They had thought of going together at first, but, having decided that she did not want to go, she told him that he must do what he wanted and, this being said, he felt relieved that she wanted him to follow his own desires and decided to go on his own.

He travelled first again to Amsterdam, then to Copenhagen, both of which were centres for youth from all over Europe at that time.

As Denmark had been the first country in Europe to legalise nudity on *all* public beaches, he spent a long time walking nude along the beach by the side of the road near Helsingør, where there were hundreds of cars passing by.

For the first time in his life, he experienced true freedom and realised that he was a person in himself, and free......

Reflections

It would have seemed to me unbelievable until now that this could happen, but I have spent 60p on this writing pad and, if it had been my last money, I would probably also have spent it, being so desperate to write this down. It follows the fact that, last night, all the scenes of my life hitherto swarmed upon my mind in an uncontrollable surge as if I was fated to fall into this swamp of memory, which consisted not merely of odd snatches of scenes and events, as we often remember but, it seemed, my whole life from start to finish, as it were, or, at any rate, from the outset until the present moment.

The fact that I had to go to college today stopped me from making a mad rush last night to get it all down on paper but, alas, due to this, I spent a nearly sleepless night and carried around feelings of guilt and confusion all day, such as I had not known for years and, throughout this morning, have not been able to concentrate steadily on a thing.

Indeed, it seems as if my whole life has, in the last few weeks, been tending towards this movement of thoughts, the first glimpse of which I had about 4.15 one afternoon, when I had left college after a dull day and started walking around streets which I did not know in my home town, the area being at the opposite end of town from where I had lived as a child. I experienced odd presentiments of things to come, mixed with all sorts of feelings from the past – like spirits hovering around ornaments on Victorian buildings which I had known in my childhood – as if I were walking in some strange atmosphere in a science-fiction film in an unexplored area of my mind.

In fact, today the truth has come upon me fully that the cause of my unhappiness goes back to long before all this. When I was sixteen years old, I lay around in parks in London in my coloured underpants and waited for young girls to look at me.

Four years earlier, at the age of twelve, and well grown and developed for my years, I used to love to take off all my clothes and walk around my room, even looking at myself in the mirror. When I took a bath, my mother would come in and

I would crouch forward so that I could wash myself at a better angle so as to let her see me.

Once, on holiday, in the north of Scotland, I wanted to go by myself further along the beach to an out-of –the-way place and swim in the nude but I didn't get very far before my parents and brother came after me, as they would not let me out of their sight for more than five minutes. That was the start of the trouble.

I had a vivid imagination at that time. For instance, I had a dream one night in which I was in a street where two old men were standing and two horses and carts passed. One of the old men said to the other, "What number are these?" (meaning registration number, as in a car). At this point, a loud voice said, "Maybe they knew more about horses and carts in the days of horses and carts than they do now", after which the dream became completely dark, followed by bright colours flashing across it and a loud voice thundered out, "The dawning of a new age". That was when I was 12 years old in 1969.

I would also take long solitary walks at night and feel that the spirit of the universe was entering into me when looking up at a starry sky. I would look out of a window and imagine that branches of trees were fated to be certain shapes.

From time to time, memories come flooding into my head and I can remember these events as if they took place only yesterday. I can even see the reflections of car headlamps on my clothes as I walked down a country road to the village on a twilit evening.

I would sit in my room for hours on end on November evenings with the window open, so that I could be in touch with the frosty universe outside, write poetry and talk to myself; I would look at cows in the fields and imagine what it would be like to be an animal and never to wear clothes; I would walk for miles and think about everything.

When I reflect on all this now, that seems to have been my real life and I wonder if I could have imagined at that time where all this would lead.

Perth, Scotland 1986

The Last Thing Before The Apocalypse

A Short Autobiography of a Teenage Nudist

I grew up in Scotland in the 1960s and moved to London when I was 16 in 1973.

Shortly after arriving in London, I saw an advertisement in *Time Out* magazine asking for people to join a nudist club in Kent.

I arrived at Eureka naturist club near Longfield early one evening.

Having never been naked in a public place before, I was a little bit embarrassed at first and was frightened to take off my clothes for about the first 10 minutes. Then, being determined to take the plunge, I took off all my clothes suddenly and very quickly and was never embarrassed about it again after that.

It had been something that I had always wanted to do since I went through puberty at the age of 11 or 12.

When undressing at night, I would have this ecstatic feeling and would walk around naked in my room for about fifteen to twenty minutes each night looking at myself in the mirror.

I also started to get sexually aroused around that time, although I didn't really understand much about that at the time as, while it might seem hard to believe now, in the small town in Scotland where I grew up, at that time, many kids didn't learn the facts of life until they were about 12 years old. No-one had explained to me what erections were although I probably had them most nights and would sit there, feeling sexually excited, listening to music like the early Pink Floyd in the dark, feeling as if I was floating in space.

I was generally considered to have grown up "too quickly", but what my parents and other people at the time didn't understand was that, probably due to my early puberty, I was in some sort of spiritual ecstasy much of the time, which came to me from a variety of sources such as listening to imaginative music, looking up at a starry sky at night, going for long walks in the country and becoming aroused by the changes in my own body.

It was also about this time that I saw pictures in a magazine of a naked primitive tribe sitting around a fire and I decided that, when I was older, or, as soon as I ever got the chance, I would travel somewhere where it was possible to be naked all the time.

My mother saw me naked regularly at that time in the home and later, when I was 15, some girls at school had stripped all the clothes off me, while they were having a prank (which I enjoyed), but my visit to Eureka was the first time that I was naked amongst total strangers. However, it didn't take me long to get used to it.

Fortunately, I was good-looking and had a good body and loved women looking at me naked and there wasn't the emphasis in the media at that time like there is nowadays about sizes of genitals and of breasts etc.

There is also a lot of paranoia nowadays about pictures of naked teenagers but I loved having my photograph taken for *Health & Efficiency* magazine, which happened several times when I was at Eureka.

However, I did find that there were several undesirable types hanging around Eureka amongst the older men, which is why I decided the next year, instead of going back to Eureka, to join Fiveacres Country Club in St. Albans, just north of London, which purported to be a more serious naturist club, and I also went to nude swimming sessions with them at Watford one night each week.

The secretary of Fiveacres also took a photo of me naked with my arms round a naked young girl, who was also a member of the club, and told me that he might also send it to *Health & Efficiency* magazine.

Unfortunately, I never saw the photograph, which I would have loved to have seen, and never discovered whether it was ever published, which I very much hoped it would be.

Earlier that year, I had also stayed for a brief period in a hippy commune which was started up by Bill Dwyer, organiser of the ill-fated Windsor Free Festival, which took place later the same year at Windsor Great Park, and ended up with the police beating everyone out of the park with truncheons.

For some reason, although that was all over the news at the time, it became quickly forgotten about.

In Bill Dwyer's commune, which was supposed to be practising free love, we all slept naked in a room at the back and there were two very sexy-looking young girls there, both aged 17, one of whom I managed to have a brief fling with.

In 1977, at the age of 20, I started travelling in Europe.

I first went to Yugoslavia on holiday, mainly because I had heard that there were lots of naturist beaches there. As well as that, I found the people there to be very friendly and particularly found the young people to be very lively. I had a brief love affair with a girl in Zagreb, who was a music student, which still stands out in my memory as being one of the most beautiful moments of my life, although our relationship didn't last very long, due to us living in different parts of Europe.

I must admit that I found the Croatian women to be very beautiful and many of them were interested in me at that time, being a foreigner.

I later returned to (what was then) Yugoslavia many times during the 1980s and my favourite place was the island of Mljet on the Croatian coast, where many young Yugoslavs went at that time as a cheap place to go where they could skinny-dip.

I also visited, amongst other places, the town of Ulcinj in Montenegro, where there was a very long stretch of unspoilt beach leading down to the Albanian border where it was possible to go nude.

I spent the next three years living and working in Holland, where the naturist movement was just starting up at that time and where there were some nudist beaches on the coast which were popular with the young people.

In 1980, I moved to what was at that time West Berlin at the time of the squatting movement. I found that many young Germans at that time were heavily into nudism and accepted nudity naturally, although sometimes it seemed to me to be contrived.

In Denmark, which was the first country in Europe to make nudity legal on all public beaches and which I visited several times between 1976 and 1980, it was also very popular among the young people at that time.

During the 1980s and 90s, I also visited nudist beaches in the Greek islands, Portugal and Fuerteventura, which is one of my favourite places and which I would strongly recommend to anyone who wants to get away from the crowd.

Unfortunately, attitudes have changed since I was younger and I have found that the young British people today, instead of accepting nudity as being natural, tend to associate it with pornography, which they are watching all the time on their computers.

I think that this is a very bad trend, but what I would advise young people today who want to go nude is to ignore everything in the media and just do it anyway. Don't listen to all the nonsense about sizes of breasts and genitals and, if you're unhappy with your body, remember that, if you go to a nudist club or beach, the chances are that there will be people of all sorts of shapes and sizes there and that it is unlikely that you will stand out.

17th October 2009

A Seventies Odyssey

After my brief love-affair in Zagreb and, having parted from the many friends I had made there in the summer of 1977 and been piled with sandwiches in the train station, I arrived in Munich the next morning, having spent the night on the overnight train.

I spent most of the time in the Englisch Garten but could only afford to buy one beer there, having not changed very much money as I only intended to spend one day there before heading north to Scandinavia.

I was served by a slightly gruff-mannered, middle-aged German who remarked, on seeing me counting a few coins together in my hands: "Not much money! Are you from England or the United States?"

I replied that I was from Scotland.

Later that evening, I met a large group of students in one of these bars in the arty district of town who thought that I was from France. I talked to one of them about Goethe. He said, "You say 'Gothy', don't you? I've heard it in London!"

When it was time for the train to depart from Copenhagen that night, I entered a carriage where there were some teenage boys who had put their shoes out and had pushed the seats together in preparation for sleeping on the train that night.

One of them asked me, "Are you going to Copenhagen?"

I replied that I was.

After having spent two more nights on overnight trains, I arrived in Stockholm two mornings later, where I made my way to the youth hostel Af Chapman which was on a boat, where I was greeted by a good-looking young Swedish girl with long, black hair and a slim figure who asked me if I was tired, which she must have noticed from the way I looked.

She told me that the guy with whom I would be sharing a room was very quiet and so I shouldn't have any problems with him.

He may have been usually very quiet but the next night proved to be an exception, when I met him in the bar on the boat, where they served glasses of very weak Swedish beer which was very expensive.

This Swedish man, who was in his early thirties, had mentioned something to me earlier about having smoked some marijuana and later arrived in the bar fairly drunk and wouldn't stop talking.

He said that he liked to go around different restaurants and not to eat very much but to drink more and talk to people (as at that time in Sweden they didn't generally have bars or pubs as such and wouldn't serve alcohol in restaurants unless someone ate something as well).

He said that he had been going around the world "looking for his special woman" and mentioned that he had been in the Yugoslav ports of Split and Dubrovnik as well as in Morocco – but he said that he didn't like it in Morocco because "they took everything".

He also went on to describe a famous café he had visited in the left bank in Paris to the amusement of two Americans who were sitting beside him. He explained, with great gusto: "Everyone was there! All the capitalists and all the communists were there! I think Picasso once painted a portrait in there! Everyone was there! I met Tom Wolfe in there!..."

At this point, one of the Americans interjected, "Who's Tom Wolfe?", in reply to which the Swede turned round and snarled, "You're Americans! You don't know anything!" He went on to say that Tom Wolfe was an American writer and asked me if I had heard of him.

I replied that I had.

One of the Americans later wrote the name "Spike Milligan" on a piece of paper and asked me, "Do you know this guy?" I replied that he was quite a famous comedian in Britain, who had mental health problems. One of them also said that he had met two people who had "said that they weren't English but from a place called Wales" and asked me if it would be OK to address a letter to them "Wales, England".

Nothing much else happened in Stockholm that summer and I made my way to The Netherlands, where I had a job lined up, via Denmark, where I stopped in the coastal resort of Skagen and wandered around in the nude on the beach there, which it was possible to do as nudity had been made legal on all Danish beaches the year before in 1976.

I arrived in The Netherlands, where I was going to start working, by overnight train from Copenhagen which passed through the north of Germany.

At the station in The Netherlands, I had to change trains and noticed with fascination that there was an automatic vending machine which sold cooked food like rissoles.

While I was waiting at the station to change trains, I met a friendly Dutch student who invited me to stay for a few nights with himself and his friends in Amsterdam before leaving for the village of Etten-Leur, near Breda in the south of The Netherlands, where I had a temporary job lined up for six weeks sorting out onions at the factory Spyer, van der Vijver en Zwanenburg bv (SVZ), which I had obtained before leaving Brighton where I had been living earlier that year. I had written to the labour departments of every EU country and also even to those of Sweden and Norway as I had been so severely depressed living alone in Brighton after my girl-friend had left me and having been faced with the prospect of unemployment and being stuck with no money that I was utterly determined to try in every way possible to find a job anywhere in Europe and start a new life, having been to Amsterdam and also to Denmark the year before and having decided at the time that I would like to live somewhere like that for longer.

The Dutch labour department had been the only one that had found me a job, which turned out to be with SVZ in Etten-Leur.

A Norwegian girl was also staying for a few nights with the Dutch students in Amsterdam. She woke up the next morning explaining that her feet were hurting her and kept talking about wanting to buy new shoes. In the end, she said that she would walk barefoot with some friends to the Flea market and buy some flip-flops there.

I arrived at Etten-Leur late that evening as it was starting to become dark, with only three guilders left in my pocket, and was taken to the sleeping quarters by the young Dutch foreman, who was very friendly.

I was housed along with about 150 mainly Irish students, who were also very friendly and outgoing, in one of about three very large tents which were lined on both sides with bunk beds.

In my dormitory, there were a group of Irish students who seemed to know each other, one of whom was a very good-looking 17-year-old boy with jet-black hair, who tended to stand out from the rest and who sang and played the guitar. He would sing songs by Bob Dylan and Leonard Cohen, Led Zeppelin's **Stairway to Heaven** and a song about Beaujolais wine. He also had some books by Hermann Hesse and Nietzsche and we all discussed literature.

There was also another Irish student who wore horn-rimmed glasses and kept talking about James Joyce and Samuel Beckett, a young English student who had also been to Stockholm and had visited the old part of the city Gamla Stan with its medieval houses and cobble-stoned streets, which was slightly reminiscent of Amsterdam, and a young French boy who seemed a bit confused about everything at first as this was probably his first time away from home.

There were also a bunch of rough Glaswegian types in the same dormitory, who always hung around together and, in one of the other dormitories, there was a young Englishman, conventionally dressed with short, dark hair, who spoke with a posh accent, whom everyone teased, referring to him as "the guy with the Oxford accent", but he took it in good part and was actually very friendly.

After I had been working there for a while, I got talking from time to time to another young Irish lad who slept at the far end of the dormitory, who tended to be always late for work through taking a long time over his breakfast. He said that his father had had something to do with a theatre in Ireland but that they had ended up in trouble for having had some nudity on stage. I wondered later if that might have been the play *Equus* by Peter Shaffer, which I had seen the year before with my girl-friend in Brighton, in which a good-looking young Irish boy and a teenage girl had stripped off on stage.

There was also a young Scottish boy in the dormitory whose father was the manager of a factory near Glasgow. He said that he had asked his father for a job before coming to work in The Netherlands, but that his father had said that the workers would play him up for being the boss's son, so, in the end, he had told him, "Get your own job, son!" He also kept talking about his girl-friend in Scotland, once saying that their relationship "had to be seen to be believed". He was in the habit of walking outside naked to go to the showers or to the toilet in the mornings and told us one morning, having come in from the showers, that a train had just gone by on the nearby railway line when he was walking from the showers to the dormitory.

There were many Yugoslavian workers among the permanent workforce in the factory, which seemed to be quite an odd coincidence at that time, as I had recently spent some time in Yugoslavia that summer.

I had given my Croatian girl-friend Elidija, whom I had met in Zagreb, my address there and was eagerly awaiting a letter from her and, so, was very glad to see one morning that a letter had arrived for me with Yugoslavian stamps. She asked me, "What does your job look like?" and also said that she thought that I would have many problems with people on my travels because I was such a "gentle, honest boy". I found her letter again many years later and all the memories came flooding back to me from that summer, which was the best time in my life.

The job finished there after six weeks and I went back to Amsterdam where I stayed in the Sleep-In, which was a place full of large dormitories where hundreds of young hippies and travellers could sleep in bunk beds, where there was always '60s music playing and where people could smoke marijuana if they wanted, and had a look around to try to find another job.

It so happened that it was at about this time that Elvis Presley died, the news of which I first heard about three days later from an English newspaper that someone must have left lying around in a café while drinking a glass of Trappist, a potent beer brewed by Belgian monks, and talking to three or four Dutch people who were sitting there, near the Spui street in the centre of Amsterdam. Many years later, I discovered that, by a strange coincidence, Elvis Presley's manager "Colonel" Tom Parker had come from the town of Breda which was the nearest town of any size to the village of Etten-Leur where I had been working that summer.

I presently found another job within a short time and without much bother through one of these temporary work agencies or "uitzendburos", as they are known in The Netherlands, in a timber factory called Bruynzeel in a place called Hembrug just outside Amsterdam. On asking for a ticket at the Centraal Station the next morning, the girl at the counter misunderstood me, thinking that I had asked for a ticket to Hamburg and told me to go to the International Section. I then explained to her that I wanted to go to a small place called Hembrug just outside Amsterdam and she gave me a ticket.

Working with me were one English guy and also a black guy from South America who was slightly eccentric.

One night, the South American guy invited us back to his place for a while. He first passed around a joint of marijuana and, after some time, offered us some rum which was 90%

proof, so we both proceeded to become very drunk and stoned quite quickly. At one point, he started moving telephones around the flat for some reason, somehow making me think about **Dr. Who**, which the English guy told me the next morning I had also said something about later when we were out in the street before asking for a drink in the bar across the road. Apparently, they had refused to serve us and, on the tram on the way back, I had kept pacing up and down and asking everyone where the Dam was, which worried the English guy because we didn't have any tickets. I didn't remember anything about this the next day, but I did remember that, when I arrived back at the Sleep-In that evening, I had met some of the young Irish students with whom I had been working in Etten-Leur and had told them that I had found a job. As a joke, I had said to them that there must be plenty of work in "these flying saucer factories that they have on Jupiter", an idea that had come to mind from a book I had read the previous year by Patrick Moore, entitled *Can You Speak Venusian?*, in which he described a number of unconventional beliefs that people had about astronomy.

The next day, the good-looking young 17-year-old with the jet-black hair, who sang and played the guitar, said to me, "We were hearing some strange things from you last night!" and I presently went for a drink with them in a small café-bar on the Leidseplein.

Another afternoon, I visited De Engelbewaarder or Literary Café, which had been, at that time, known as a meeting place for writers in Amsterdam. There I met a professor of sociology with one of his students. The sociology professor asked me what books I was interested in reading, to which I replied that I had recently read a book by the Norwegian novelist Knut Hamsun. He misheard what I had said and replied, "No, I've read Hunter Thompson, but..."

"No, Knut Hamsun... He was a Norwegian writer..."

"Oh, Knut Hamsun! No, Knut Hamsun is one of these writers who are sold in book clubs. It's like Hermann Hesse..."

"Oh, yes, I like Hermann Hesse as well!"

At this, the professor seemed even more annoyed and said that he "liked to read about the real world".

I replied that perhaps it was a different side of reality.

At this, his face contorted into a grimace and he went on to say, "Yes, but writers like Hermann Hesse and Knut Hamsun seem to write about people who don't quite know who they are....."

I was totally nonplussed by this and did not know what to reply to such a statement as it seemed to me that writers like Hermann Hesse and Knut Hamsun were unique in that they were, at least, trying to find out who they were and what was in their subconscious whereas most people didn't seem to be even aware that there was anything wrong in the first place.

I asked the young student what he thought about this, to which he replied rather embarrassedly, "I agree with my teacher!" at which the professor turned round and said, "You don't have to!"

After a while, the student started to become more and more drunk and began to describe his experiences in the gay bars and clubs during a recent visit he had made to West Berlin.

The professor appeared to be quite taken aback at his student's sudden and unexpected admission of his homosexuality.

I asked the student what it had been like there, at which the professor suggested that it would have been *cruel*.

The student turned round and replied, "No, it was good because there were many opportunities for people to meet each other who wanted to....."

He then went on to say that there was one club where homosexuals met each other to dance but that it had been spoiled recently because they had also begun letting in heterosexuals.

As an instinctive reaction to this, the professor and myself both interjected, "Why?"

The student didn't seem to be able to give a very clear answer to that question.

The student and the professor also asked me if I had read Christopher Isherwood. I had been introduced to Christopher Isherwood by a woman in Brighton earlier that year but had not taken up her advice to read him, *not* being interested in homosexuality.

They both recommended that I should read **Christopher and His Kind**, which they explained was about his experiences in West Berlin.

After a while, the professor departed and I was left alone with the student who, for some reason, was determined to buy me a Jägermeister, a German liqueur of which I had not heard at that time.

Although it is generally unusual for someone to buy a German drink in The Netherlands, I somehow always associated Jägermeister after that with that summer in Amsterdam, along with the song **Hotel California** by The Eagles, which was being played everywhere at that time.

He kept saying to me that I had a very nice face, at which I laughed embarrassedly and smiled at the waitress, a nice-looking girl with jet-black hair, who asked me with some concern, "Does he bother you?"

I said, "No, it's all right!" Then I drank the Jägermeister and went out.

I had saved some money from having worked at my first two jobs in The Netherlands and had itchy feet again, so planned to go to Norway, to travel right up to the far north of Scandinavia and also to Finland, as I had been looking at all of this on an Inter-Rail map.

Earlier that year, I had met an Irish girl in London who had also been up there with Inter-Rail and said that she had spent a long time in Lappland.

In my ignorance at that time, I had asked her, "Where about *is* Lappland exactly?", thinking that Lappland was a country. She put me on the right track by explaining that Lappland was the name given to the far northern part of Scandinavia, which is north of the Arctic Circle. Somehow, I had the urge to travel as far north as possible.

She had also said to me that Finland was wonderful, although she didn't say exactly what was so wonderful about it and I was later to find that there wasn't really much to see or do there.

It was on the same visit to London, before meeting her, that I was looking in a bookshop for something interesting to read as I had run out of reading material at that time.

Amongst the Picador books, I came across a copy of **Victoria** by Knut Hamsun, a writer who was new to me at that time, and bought it as it as it attracted my attention, probably mainly because his writing was compared to that of Hermann Hesse on the cover. I found myself to be quite emotionally moved by this romantic love story which had been written shortly before the turn of the 20th Century and resolved after that to read some more of his works which were to take my mind off my boring and depressing way of life during that period and I would read them on the bus to and from the paper sack factory where I was working in Hove while desperately trying to save some money with a view to moving abroad.

After **Victoria**, I read first **Hunger** and then **Mysteries**.

I could relate quite easily to **Hunger**, having been unemployed and having gone through difficulties myself recently, a situation which I had resolved to put an end to as the hero of **Hunger** does at the end of the book when he escapes his period of starvation and paranoia in Oslo by signing on a Russian merchant ship and fleeing to America – and I also liked the excitable style in which it was written, which was probably similar to how I myself would have described such an episode.

I found **Mysteries** to be highly imaginative and, as the title would suggest, mysterious. I had become bewitched by Hamsun's writings and needed something like that at that time to transport me into another world and push my own problems into the background.

Fortunately, at that time, I didn't bother to read introductions to books, or I might have been put off. After having finished reading **Victoria**, **Hunger** and **Mysteries**, I was very surprised and somewhat disturbed to learn on skimming through the introduction to **Hunger** that such an imaginative and sensitive writer as Hamsun, who had written such brilliant novels in his youth, who had seemed to display such an insight into human nature and who had had such an enormous influence on 20th Century European – and, to some extent, also American – literature had lived on to a very old age and had later supported the Nazis as an 80-year-old man - and could only conclude that he must have been senile at the time, which tends to be an accepted opinion depending on whom one chooses to believe.

However, I have recently come to the conclusion that it may have been the case that a dark side of his personality came out in the end as his novels are full of very intense mood swings, perhaps due to the fact that he grew up in the far north of Norway where it is light for half the year and dark for half the year. As Carl Jung said, "The brighter the light, the darker the shadow"......

One day, while at the Centraal Station in Amsterdam, I met a German girl who asked me to lend her some money to go back home and who gave me her address in Essen. I didn't really expect to get the money back or to see her again but thought that I would make my way to Essen with my Inter-Rail card and try to look her up before travelling on to Norway.

On arrival in Essen, I bought a map at the station and tried to look for the street. While looking for the house number, in the same street, I met a young guy with long hair, who told me that he was a gardener, with some of his friends. It turned out that the girl I had met at the station in Amsterdam wasn't really living at that address, so the young gardener and his friends invited me to stay at their place for a few days.

Nothing much happened there except that they played the record **Even in the Quietest Moments** by Supertramp, which had been released that year and which I heard there for the first time. I thought that the last track on the second side, entitled **Fool's Overture**, sounded strange with the voice of Winston Churchill on the record.

On leaving Essen, I met a German teacher at the station with some teenage French pupils whom he had been teaching to speak German. After talking to him for a while and also trying to talk to a young boy, who was one of his pupils, the teacher said to me that the boy spoke quite good German but that he would need to go to England to learn English.

He asked me if I had ever been to France, to which I replied that I had been in Paris once. When he proceeded to enquire of me whether I thought that I would go there again, I said that I thought that it would be unlikely.

He went on to ask me, "You don't like the French?", but, in fact, the real reason was due to problems with the language.

On the train, I met a young French sailor who was, at present, living in Belgium but who told me that he was also travelling around the world because he didn't like his own country.

He was also going to Norway to see a girl that he had only met once before and didn't know what to expect. He said that it had been the first time that he had done this, i.e. to go on such a long journey in search of a girl and that he had decided to do so on an odd whim.

After a while, he pointed to his throat and said that something was "bad for the troth" (mispronouncing the word "throat"). He presently went on to ask me, "If you have a pain in the troth, is it called 'truthache'?"

An older German was sitting drawing a picture on his lap of a crucifixion in the mountains. When someone asked him what he was drawing, he replied, "Crucifixion in die Bergen". A girl asked him if he meant the town of Bergen in Norway, to which someone replied that "Bergen" meant "mountains" in German.

On reaching the Danish border, a black guy who was travelling in the same carriage was told by one of the German border guards that he should have had a transit visa to travel through Germany and he asked me for his coat before being led away somewhere on the train. Perhaps they thought that he was a terrorist, or something.....

When we reached Copenhagen, the French sailor and myself both agreed that it was a good place to go in the summer when there was a friendly atmosphere with lots of young people but that, at that time of year, it didn't seem to be so good there and it was cold....

We took the boat-train across to Sweden and headed towards the small town in Norway, just a few stations over the border, where the French sailor was planning to meet this girl that he had met somewhere once.

After we had passed Gothenburg, a middle-aged Norwegian, dressed in a suit, who was quite drunk, came on the train and started talking to us. He and the French sailor had a conversation for some time about women. The Norwegian had two bottles of spirits in a bag with him and the Frenchman turned round and warned him, "You'd better watch out for the border guards because it is not allowed to have alcohol in this country!", meaning that it wasn't allowed to drink alcohol openly in a public place in Sweden, but I explained that perhaps the border guards wouldn't come on the train between Sweden and Norway, at which the Norwegian turned round and said to him, "And now *he* can tell you something that *you* don't know!"

Before leaving the train, the drunken Norwegian gave the French sailor his address and offered us both a job at some hamburger place which he owned in a small town or village a few stops before the Frenchman's destination.

We arrived there late at night and things didn't go well between the young French sailor and the girl who hadn't expected to see him.

That night, all the hotels were full and were very expensive, so the sailor spent the night at the police station while I spent the night in the waiting room at the railway station where the station-master locked me in and let me stay.

On the way back to the station that night, I noticed that there was a plaque on the wall of one building to say that the writer Henrik Ibsen had lived there.

The next morning, when I met the French sailor again, he said that he was annoyed because, at the police station, they had taken his passport and he also suggested that we should go to see this drunken man we had met on the train, who had offered us both a job and had said that we could stay at his place.

I said to him, "Maybe he is a homosexual!", at which he laughed and replied, "Well, I've always got *you* to protect me!"

I decided instead to travel on to Oslo and so we parted company that morning.

On the train journey to Oslo, I captured my first glimpse of the spectacular Norwegian scenery, with mist rising over the mountains, while I talked to a good-looking, blonde-haired young Norwegian girl on the train.

In Oslo, I visited the Edvard Munch museum but nothing much else happened there except that I had a cup of coffee and wrote a postcard in the cafe at the station, where I seem to remember there being a mural of sleighs driving reindeer on the wall.

As there weren't many railways in Norway, I would have to travel through Sweden to reach Narvik, which was my destination, as that was the end of the train-line, so I took the train from Oslo to Stockholm that night, which was full of young backpackers like myself.

The next afternoon, I took the train heading north out of Stockholm just as it was starting to get dark. I didn't have much money, so could only afford to have one cup of coffee in the buffet car on the train, where I talked for a while to a young Swede.

A woman came down the corridor of the train selling lottery tickets and I looked at the names of the stations outside the window as it became darker and we travelled much farther north than the northernmost tip of Scotland or anywhere I had ever been before in my life.

Late that night, we arrived in the town of Gavle, where I would have to change trains before heading to the iron-mining town of Kiruna in the north of Sweden, where I would have to change again for Narvik.

While waiting at the station in Gavle, I sat and talked to a young Swede who complained about the alcohol restrictions in Sweden, saying that "it was much better in the old days" and who also talked about *The Fabulous Furry Freak Brothers*, an old hippy comic from the 1960s.

He also said that he thought that it was a strange time of year to be travelling to Narvik, as it was too late to see the midnight sun and would also be too early to see the Northern Lights, which Knut Hamsun had described to brilliantly in his novel *Pan*, which, by coincidence, I had read on a train from Stockholm to Gothenburg earlier that summer at the same time as my Croatian girl-friend Elidija had read it.

The train pulled out of Gavle at some time late that night and headed north towards the iron-mining town of Kiruna.

In Norway, there would have been spectacular scenery, with fjords and mountains coming down to the sea but, in Sweden, there was nothing but hundreds of miles of forests in all directions.

The tourist leaflets advised people not to go out into the forests in case they got lost.

After quite a long time on the train, eventually there were signs saying "Arctic Circle" in several languages with a row of stones marking out the circle on both sides of the railway line and receding into the distance.

The train reached the iron-mining town of Kiruna some time early that afternoon, where I waited at the station and talked to two young girls who were only wearing thin blouses in spite of the fact that it was much colder there than I had ever known it to be even in Scotland in the winter.

One could see iron mines on all sides and some miners returning home from work later in the afternoon as it started to become dark.

For some reason, it reminded me of a ramshackle town from a Western film with so many wooden houses spread out over such a large area.

The tourist leaflets stated that much of the world's iron supplies came from there. What they did not state, and what I also did not know at that time, was that this was where the Germans had got most of their iron from during the war, which they had taken out through the Norwegian port of Narvik, which was only a short train journey away. When someone told me this later, the next year, I was rather shocked and surprised that Sweden's socialist government had done this, but then I supposed that every country must have had a dark side to its history at some time.

Axel Munthe, in his book **The Story of San Michele**, which I was to read many years later, described some sort of hallucinatory reverie in which the Laplanders had said that they were terrified of the train passing along the railway line, which had just been built at that time to transport the iron, because they had thought that it was a giant snake. Perhaps that was some sort of portent of things to come.....

The train pulled into Narvik that night and we all piled into the youth hostel.

The next day, I wandered around the ramshackle town where there was nothing much to do and walked down to the beach at the foot of the mountains. The *Let's Go: Europe* guide stated that there was a beach there "if anyone was mad enough to go for a swim". Nobody went for a swim and I was the only person standing there.

That night, I went for a drink in the only bar in town in a hotel where all the foreigners gathered. There was one Dutch woman in her mid-twenties and a Swedish man who was probably in his early thirties.

The Dutch woman started saying that she didn't like Germans, to which the Swedish man kept asking her, rather sarcastically, in way of reply, if that was because of the Second World War.

She said, "No! My father has a wound in his leg, but – for instance, one time, there were all these Germans on the beach in Holland, talking very loudly as if to attract attention to everyone that 'We are *German*!'"

At that time, I had heard many Dutch people talking about hating the Germans and had thought that they were living in the past, having met many young Germans myself whom I had thought were nice people and very friendly, but it was only later, having lived in West Berlin for some time, that I started to modify my opinion somewhat.....

By this time, the Dutch woman was starting to become quite drunk and kept shouting out that "Sweden has the best social system in the world!", to which the Swedish man kept replying, "You don't have to go *on* about it!"

She invited me to come and sleep with her in her car, but I thought that it would be much too cold.....

The day after that, I decided to head towards Finland and took the train, this time during the day, through some quite spectacular Norwegian mountainous scenery, also through the north of Sweden, past the iron mines again, then through the north of Finland and down towards Helsinki.

While I was travelling on the train through Finland, at one point, all the foreign travellers were wondering at which town the train was going to stop. At one station, there was a sign saying "Ravintola", meaning "restaurant" in Finnish, and a young Englishman on the train, who tended to show his ignorance about things, particularly of foreign languages, announced to everyone that the name of the station was "Rav-in-*tol*-a", pronouncing it wrongly.

I found that there was nothing much to see in Finland and that Helsinki was just a dull, grey city where people seemed very cold and distant.

At one point, in the railway station in Helsinki, I noticed that there was a sign above one of the windows advertising tickets to the U.S.S.R. It had occurred to me before I started travelling that I might take a day trip to Leningrad, which it would have been possible to do, getting a visa at the border, except that I found that I did not have enough money to do so.

I took the boat back to Stockholm that night. There was a stormy sea and I was seasick for the only time in my life.

On reaching Stockholm, I took the train back down through the south of Sweden, again through Denmark and the north of Germany, back to Amsterdam.....

On arrival in Amsterdam, I booked into the Eben Haezer Christian Youth Hostel as it was the cheapest place to stay in town.

One afternoon, a good-looking Swedish girl came out of the shower with wet hair in bare feet.

I must have smiled at her without noticing because she smiled back at me and then sat down at a small table opposite me and we started talking.

While we were sitting there talking, one of the Christians who ran the hostel came round and handed out one of these simple leaflets which attempted to explain Christianity.

The Swedish girl started to read it and seemed to think that it made quite good sense – perhaps not having come from a religious background herself – but what she probably wouldn't have realised was that Christians have generally tended to have very strict ideas about certain aspects of life, particularly marriage and sexual relationships.

In any case, I didn't see her again after that.

Another night, I went out for a drink in a café-bar with a group of German girls, who lived in West Berlin. They told me that they had some problems with the people who were running the hostel because they had made some sort of joke about religion in response to a speech which had been given by one of the Christians who worked there, which they would probably have found patronising.

They reacted to this the next morning by placing a notice on the board at the entrance, containing a poem, starting with the line "Jesus loves you!   So do I!.....", written in a way as if it was intended to be sexually provocative.

One of the girls said that, after that, she had heard a woman working at the hostel exclaiming, "These German girls make problems for us!"

I also didn't see them again after that.

During that week, I obtained work from a temporary agency in another onion factory, where the foreman was fairly insolent.

One evening, having arrived back in the centre of Amsterdam tired after a hard day's work, I went to the Kosmos club, a meditation/youth centre where no alcohol was sold but where it was acceptable to smoke marijuana if one wanted to and where there was also a sauna and sometimes live music and cultural events.

After I had left the place that night, I saw someone with short, dark hair standing on the corner wearing a duffle coat and, to begin with, I was unsure whether it was a man or a woman.

I assumed at first that it was someone needing help with directions and asked this person if they were looking for somewhere.

It turned out to be a woman and she said, "No," but went on to add, in a sort of faltering voice, "but you were staring, when I was sitting with my friends in the Kosmos....." I replied that I had not been conscious of staring at her and she went on to say that I had looked very lonely.

I asked her where she was from. She said that she was from Germany, sounding slightly embarrassed, and it turned out that her name was Susanne.

She also told me later that she "had never done something like that before", meaning to approach a man like that, and then I remembered that my Croatian girl-friend Elidija had said something along similar lines that summer.

We wandered around the streets for a while and talked about all sorts of things that night. She told me that she had also travelled up to the far north of Scandinavia and mentioned that she had had the feeling all the time that she had kept wanting to travel farther and farther north and always to go farther and said that she thought that everyone had that feeling at some time when travelling.

The next day, we came to the Kabul Hotel.

We started looking at rooms and, when we came to look at the double rooms, I noticed that Susanne seemed interested.

She said, "I'd like to share a room with you!"

We got together that afternoon, but, much to my regret, perhaps due to my youth and nervousness at the time, I found that I was unable to satisfy her. I always thought of this as having been a great disappointment as it seemed to me that our relationship should have lasted longer and that it might have done if it hadn't been for that.

In the end, she got up suddenly, burst into tears and went into a sulk. However, we still remained firm friends after that and, the next morning, she bought some bread and peanut butter which we ate for breakfast on a disused barge on one of the canals.

We then walked past some hippy houseboats, painted in bright colours, which were a left-over from the 1960s.

On the side of one of the houseboats were painted the following lines from a poem by William Blake:

> "He who binds to himself a joy
> Does the winged life destroy;
> But he who kisses a joy as it flies
> Lives in eternity's sunrise."

Another boat had painted on it the words "PARADISE NOW" in bright letters. I later discovered that "Paradise Now" had been the name of some sort of hippy political movement in Amsterdam in the late 1960s.

Past the houseboats, we came to De Engelbewaarder or Literary Café where I had had the conversation with the professor of sociology and the young student before travelling to Norway.

I ordered two glasses of Trappist, a potent brew produced by monks in Belgium, which I had tried several times before in Amsterdam.

We sat at the back of the table where the newspapers were laid out and talked for a while.

Susanne said that she was thinking of learning one of the Scandinavian languages and that it would probably be Norwegian. I said, "So you'll get into this Knut Hamsun!" "Was that a writer?" she asked, apparently not having heard of him.

She also went on to say that she had had some sort of nervous breakdown at one time and had been hospitalised but only for one day. She also told me that she had worked with R. D. Laing, which was a strange coincidence, as a woman I knew quite well in Brighton had also met R. D. Laing and another friend of mine in England had undergone therapy with Laing and had known him personally. By an even stranger coincidence, Susanne and this friend of mine were to meet each other out of the blue years later in London (they hadn't known each other before) but didn't get on with each other for some reason and, by all accounts, had some sort of blazing row.

I had thought that Susanne would have been drunk from the Trappist, not being used to it, but it seemed to have had very little effect on her.

The next day, we watched a hippy guy playing a flute in the Vondelpark and later sat down at a place where there were some buses with the letters "U.S.S.R." written on the side.

Susanne remarked, "Look at these buses from Russia! Isn't that amazing! But I think that they are from Finland, because they have stickers with the letters 'SU', meaning 'Suomi'...", Suomi being the native name for Finland. I suggested that the letters "SU" might stand for "Soviet Union", but she didn't seem to take that idea seriously.

After a while, Susanne became distracted by something going on to her left-hand side, of which I was not aware, as I was sitting at her right-hand side, looking in the other direction.

It turned out that a middle-aged German couple, who were drunk, were poking fun at some old tramp who was not wearing shoes. Susanne went on to say that she always felt ashamed of being German because of incidents like that and also went on to speak about some people she had met who had been to the Anne Frank Huis and had described the horrors that they had seen in there.

She asked me what book I was reading, referring to a large, thick book which I had in the pocket of my Army jacket and which someone in the youth hostel had mistaken for a telephone directory.

It was **The Diary of a Drug Fiend** by Aleister Crowley, which I was reading, not out of any interest either in drugs or in the occult, but because I liked Crowley's sense of humour.

Susanne and I parted later that afternoon, as I took the train to Tiel, a small town near where I would be starting to work in the Veluco food canning factory at the village of Geldermalsen, but we promised to keep in contact.

I still had my Inter-Rail card, which I had used on my tour of Scandinavia, and took further advantage of this by using it half-price in The Netherlands for the journey to Tiel.

On the train, I started talking to a young Dutch guy, who was wearing hippy clothes, after asking directions. On hearing us talking in English, an Australian businessman came over and started a conversation with us, as he was also going to Tiel on business and wanted to find out more about the place.

It turned out that there were also mostly Irish students working at the Veluco factory in Geldermalsen and there were two Scottish guys who were going around doing odd jobs so as to get together enough money to travel to different places. One of them wanted to go to South America for some native festival which he expected to be wild and Dionysian.

As I still had some time left on my Inter-Rail card, I decided to visit Berlin that weekend. I don't know exactly what I expected of that city, except that I had heard that it was also a centre for young people from all over Europe – and I also thought that, if I went there, I would visit the East – just out of curiosity.

I arrived in West Berlin that night, having struck up a conversation with an older German couple on the train. The man said that, when he was younger, he had started travelling like me and had ended up in South Africa.

When his wife asked me where I would stay, he turned round and replied, "There are enough young people in Berlin!" I managed to stay with a young guy and his girl-friend whom I met in a bar.

I spent most of the time that weekend in the bars around the Savignyplatz talking to the young crowd who gathered there and heard the sounds of Led Zeppelin's **Kashmir** echoing and reverberating throughout the place.

In one of the bars, there was an old British telephone kiosk and there I kept meeting an English busker with waist-length hair and a beard, who went around asking people for coins.

He said to me, "It's a corner of a foreign field, you know!"

I replied, "Is it?"

Late that Sunday afternoon, I went through the checkpoint to the East at the Underground station at Friedrichstrasse.

I was slightly nervous at first in the way that most Western people, at that time, tended to be apprehensive about the Russians. Perhaps because of the way I may have looked, I was taken into a room on the way through and searched. When I came out on to the street at the other side, I didn't realise at first that I was, in fact, already in East Berlin.

I spent most of the few hours I was there in cafés drinking vodka and talking to students.

On the way back, I found it hard to find directions to Friedrichstrasse. One woman I asked kept saying to me, "You must go to the *Check*point – Charlie!" (as if I was looking for the checkpoint and my name was Charlie).

Eventually, I managed to find Friedrichstrasse and the way back to the West and to the Bahnhof Zoo just in time for my overnight train back to The Netherlands.

When I arrived back to start work again at Geldermalsen, the young Dutch guy in charge saw me coming back with a rucksack and some bags and gave me a lift.

He asked me where I had been.

I said, "Berlin!"

He asked, "East or West?"

I replied, "Both!"

I started work the same day as I was still young and able to do things like that.

A short time after this, the work at the Veluco factory in Geldermalsen finished and I returned to Amsterdam to look for another job and to renew my residence permit, which had expired after three months.

I was offered work by another temporary agency or "uitzendburo" and made my way to renew my residence permit at the main police station in Amsterdam, opposite the Milky Way (Melkweg) club, outside which young hippies would stand smoking joints at night, with the police looking on and not paying any attention.

When I explained that I wished to renew my residence permit, the gruff, middle-aged, grey-haired policeman behind the desk gave me a dirty look and asked, "Why?" I probably wasn't very articulate in giving my reasons and, when he asked me where I was working, I gave him the name of the uitzendburo, at which he abruptly snapped that I must have "a *normal* job *–no* uitzendburo!" and handed me back my passport – and that was that.

I had heard from some people that it was easier for someone to have their residence permit renewed in Utrecht than in Amsterdam – so, with that in mind, I made my way to Utrecht that afternoon.

As I had nowhere to stay that night and did not have much money with me, I started talking to a young student with shoulder-length blond hair, who let me stay with him at a house which he shared with a young acupuncturist, who had inherited the house from his father.

The next day, I managed to find a temporary job stacking books on shelves for a book club and went to the police station the next morning to renew my residence permit, which turned out to be a lot less hassle than in Amsterdam. On the same day, it was reported on the news that three Baader-Meinhof terrorists had been found dead in prison in Germany and that the German businessman Hans Martin Schleyer had been murdered.

I started to work at the book club on the Thursday of that week and noticed that, on the shelves, were a variety of books in Dutch, including translations of works by Nietzsche and Knut Hamsun.

I ended up only working there for two days as, that Friday, I was offered another job in a printing press, which was better paid.

After having made the necessary arrangements to start work there the next week, I had a few glasses of beer in one of the four student café-bars near the Dom cathedral, opposite the bar where I had met the young student with whom I was staying, from where I heard two professors of astronomy talking to each other very loudly in English at great length.

I also noticed that, hanging around one of the other bars, next to De Vriendschap, where I was having a drink, were two

Dutchmen with red hair and beards who reminded me of Vincent van Gogh.

While working at the printing press van Boekhoven Bosch the next week, I had a good look around the place and noticed that they printed everything from all the Dutch telephone directories and railway timetables to a book of poems by Pablo Neruda and even a pornographic magazine.

I came to know a young German who was working there and who was interested in psychology. He was into bio-energetics and gave me a book about body language by a follower of Wilhelm Reich one night when he came round to the house where I was staying. He said that he thought that I must be having problems living in a foreign country but didn't give any reason for saying that. He also said that he sometimes had problems being accepted by the young Dutch people because he had been brought up very strictly at a boarding school in Germany and went on to add, "and there is also the *history* of Germany... and the *history* of Holland... which is... *better...*"

That Sunday, I met a sexy-looking Dutch girl with shoulder-length black hair, who was wearing a bright red top, in the bar next to De Vriendschap, where I had previously noticed the two Dutchmen with red hair and beards, whom I had thought looked like Vincent van Gogh.

After we had been talking for some time, I became slightly drunk and started talking loudly and was given a strange look from the barman, at which she laughed and motioned to me not to attract so much attention.

We left shortly after that and I spent the night with her. Before we made love, while she was sitting up in bed in her underwear, she started snorting some speed. She then asked me if I had taken any drugs, to which I replied that I had not taken any drugs other than the odd smoke of marijuana occasionally, which she said she found hard to believe.

The next morning, I started to go down with a cold and she suggested that I should stay with her instead of going into work, but I insisted that I would have to go to work as I was frightened that I would have to leave The Netherlands and return to the U.K., where there would be nothing going for me, if I lost my job. This created a misunderstanding between us which, unfortunately, ended our relationship.

After that, she said that she had lost interest in men and was only interested in women – and the last time I saw her she was with a lesbian-friend with cropped-short, black hair, who acted in a very cold, masculine manner and who was very unfriendly towards me.....

It so happened that, later that week, I had to take a few days off work because I had gone down with the flu and, due to that, I lost my job at the printing press.

The acupuncturist, with whom I was staying, asked me if he could stick some needles in me, which he did but, afterwards, I was unsure as to whether or not this had had any effect.

At about this time, a bearded professor of botany from the University came to visit, who said that he had been in Scotland and that the Glaswegians had said to him, "There's only one good thing that comes out of Edinburgh and that's the train to Glasgow....."

One night, I was surprised to see a young man whom I did not know in the house. It turned out that he had let himself in using a hook which had been tied to the inside of the letter box. I must admit that it rather amazed me at the time that they would trust people as much as that.

Another night, I heard some strange noises coming from the kitchen, as if someone was moving about there, and thought that there might be a burglar. I went rushing up the stairs to the bedroom of the blond-haired student, whose name was Ben, and explained my anxiety. He exclaimed, "Oh, no, it is mouses! It is mouses! I am sure of it!"

They had various records in the house, which included Pink Floyd's **Ummagumma**, King Crimson's **In the Court of the Crimson King**, Bob Dylan's **Highway 61 Revisited** and **The Songs of Leonard Cohen**.

One afternoon, I listened to Dylan's **Highway 61 Revisited** after which I started to play **The Songs of Leonard Cohen**. Some children at the window stood there laughing and seemed particularly curious when they heard me speaking English.

After this, they would let themselves into the house from time to time and, on one occasion, they pulled the curtain away when I was having a shower and giggled with laughter when they saw me there.

Due to the fact that I had been ill for a few days, and had lost my job at the printing press van Boekhoven Bosch, I found another job at a bakery for a different agency.

I started working there on the night shift. On the first night, shortly after I had started work, a young Dutch boy, who was also working there temporarily, who seemed quite stoned, in bare feet in sandals, kept exclaiming to me, "It is *very* maddening! It is *very* maddening!", perhaps due to all the noise of the machines.

A short walk from the house in the Wagendwaarstraat, where I was staying, was the Wilhelminapark, where there was a statue of the old Dutch Queen Wilhelmina, who was the mother of Queen Juliana, who was still Queen of The Netherlands at that time.

On the other side of the Wilhelminapark was a bar called Jan Primus, which sold about 150 different types of beer from all over the world, including Tsing Tao beer from China, which I tried out of curiosity, Theakston's Olde Peculier from Yorkshire, England and also the usual selection of Trappist beers, brewed by Belgian monks, both Dubbel and Trippel.

One night there, I met a young Dutch girl with long, dark hair and glasses, who was rather drunk, with some of her friends.

This led to another encounter and, by this time, I was becoming quite glad that so many young ladies on the Continent were showing interest in me, which I found to be very different from my experience in the UK. Over the next three years, I would also have been with a girl from Israel, another German girl, another Dutch girl, a prostitute from North Africa, an Irishwoman in Amsterdam, another Yugoslavian girl who came to see me in The Netherlands and a girl from Finland whom I later went to visit in Stockholm – but I was to realise many years later that Elidija was really the one I loved the best and it is one of the greatest regrets of my life that I didn't keep in contact with her or try to see her again – or was it better just to have kept what happened in my mind as a pleasant memory of that summer? I will never know. All I know is that she was to haunt me for the rest of my life and from time to time the memories would all come flooding back to me.

I took this girl, whom I had met in the café-bar Jan Primus, back to the house where I was staying and started to make love to her, in the middle of which Epi the acupuncturist and Ben the blond-haired student walked in, about which they later showed some annoyance.

The next night, she also visited me and I put on the record **Ummagumma** by Pink Floyd and started dancing around in a way which she said she found strange, along with the music, and which frightened her, but I couldn't understand why she found this so disturbing.

After a while, she quickly headed for the door and ran with full speed up the dark street.

The next morning, the doorbell rang and there stood Susanne, who had suddenly arrived unannounced. I had not been expecting her, but had had a dream about her the night before.

Blaigowrie, Scotland 2002